Blac

Ge

This book is dedicated to my mother Linda Gregory for birthing me, my sister Halassi Masaai for her encouragement and for challenging me to write a book. Also, for my nephew Demme' for being the inspiration in a world so bleak, and Decorlan, Maya, Kente' and Aria. I love you all too.

Black Devil-Blue Eyes

Table of contents

BLACK DEVIL, BLUE EYES

Black Devil-Blue Eyes

Chapter One
How in the fuck?

How did I get into this mess? Just six or so months ago I was swimming in the crystal blue water playing with dolphins; now I'm inmate 22036G. The funny thing is, I got an idea how, but it's the why that's a little puzzling. I mean, she was so beautiful. Fucked up thing though, she was black. I always thought that we as black people, for the most part, looked out for each other. I mean I heard about that crab syndrome shit, but I figured if I stayed away from jealous ass niggas and I'd be alright. Wrong, wrong, wrong.

See, all my life I always got shit from white people. My pops used to call them white devils. I used to laugh like fuck. He never did say why, that's just what he called them. From the little boy Anthony Danzio that used to kick the shit out of me in 6th grade, to that bitch teacher I had in 5th grade named Mrs. Jepsen. The old hag used to make me sit away from the class faced backward whenever I talked in class. Sometimes I didn't even have to do shit. Now, I'm not saying I never did shit growing up, but I think the times I did to the times I didn't ratio was very unproportioned.

Anyways, back to the story, ah yes, her name was Conchita. Imagine Beyoncé, but with a bigger ass, with jet black hair and skin to match. Craziest shit though was that she wasn't even black. I mean, African-American. She was black though. I used to think that there were different types of races, but there aren't. You're either a person of color, or you're a non-colored person. Sounds weird, right? I know. See the way I figured it out is this, go to Brazil, and you'll see brown and black Brazilians and even white Brazilians. Places like Germany, England, and Asia are no different. I mean, when it boils down to it, it's colored skin or non-colored skin. That's just a theory of mine. I could be wrong, I have been many times, but fuck all that, back to Conchita. Never in a million years did I think she would do me up like she did, but to explain this whole fiasco, I'd have to go back to my humble beginnings.

Chapter Two
The rewind

The year was 1997, and the basketball court was always the hangout place for Deondre and me.

"Yo, throw the fucking ball!" Deondre said in his tough guy voice. He would always try to act like Big Pun or Fat Joe. He felt like he had to say everything with an attitude.

"Man, stop trying to act black all the time," I said with affirmation.

"Whatchu mean?" Deondre answered back with a puzzled look on his face. "Fool, I am black," he sharply added. These were the regular spats we would have at the b-ball court down on 140th and Lennox.

"Look, just because you tan and shit doesn't mean you black. Get it right boy," I said with conviction.

"Hey, Puerto Ricans are a people of African, Taino's and European decent mutha-fucka, but fuck all that!" he replied loudly. Then he continued, "Yo, let's steal a car. I want to see Rhonda tonight. She said she isn't scared to gimme' the pussy, and I don't wanna catch the "R" train. Last week I got chased home by those mutha-fucking Latin Squad boys after I got off the "R," he said with a mix of fear and confidence.

"Again?" I said with reservation. "Man, I ain't trying to go to Rikers' for some dumb shit," I said sternly. Deondre hated when I knocked his ideas, and I could see him getting pissed while I was talking.

"Man, stop being a pussy! Yo, if I get stopped I'll tell the jakes I stole the car, and you were just hitching a ride. You gotta' learn to lie nigga," he said. Figuring that made sense, we dapped up and I agreed to meet him at the park at eight.

When I got back to the playground the sky was turning dark. I knew my mom would be wondering where the hell I was at, but I told Deondre I would go, so I kept my word. I don't know if it was the dinner I ate, lunch from school or the fact I was about to get into a stolen car, but my stomach was bubbling like crazy. I arrived at the park exactly at eight, and after thirty minutes I began to worry. As soon as I turned to go home, that's when I heard Deondre's voice behind me.

"Yo pussy!" he shouted. I hated when he called me that, it was annoying as fuck.

"Fuck you, nigga! I almost left your stupid ass. You always late," I barked.

"Man fuck all that," he said. "I got some bud to smoke on the way there," he said with a half-cocked grin on his face.

Once we got into the car I smothered my hand over the vent to see if the heat was blowing. Deondre always stole the most raggedy piece of shit on the street.

"No heat?" I grumbled. It felt like we were driving for hours, but I knew it was the joint that we had smoked making me think that. As we drove, I looked out the window to admire the view over the bridge. The skyline was beautiful. All the lights looked like stars that had hit the city. While I was taking in the sight, I was abruptly interrupted by Deondre's bellowing voice.

"Hey fool, you heard me?" he said sounding slightly agitated.

"Naw, I was zoning out," I responded back lazily.

"I asked if you wanted to stop at Mickey D's," he said.

"Hell yeah, but I only got a dollar on me," I replied.

"Man, fuck that shit! I got you," he said empathetically. Then we sped to the nearest McDonalds, ordered off the dollar menu and bolted back into the street like MacGyver on a mission.

When we pulled up to Rhonda's project building, I could tell Deondre's train of thought was starting to wan.

"Yo, I'm gonna be upstairs no longer than forty-five minutes, so listen to the radio or something. If the jakes roll up on you, tell em' you waiting on yo' pops," he said.

"Yeah whatever, just hurry the fuck up, I ain't trying to be in this stuffy ass car all night," I replied.

While sitting in that hunter green cutlass, it made me feel older than I was. I looked in amazement at the few people outside that were oblivious that I was in a stolen car. Either they knew and didn't care or didn't know at all. Bored as hell, I turned on the radio and scrolled the knob to the oldies station. Listening to oldies always made me think about times when I was a little kid. The radio must've been reading my mind because every song they played was my favorite.

After thirty minutes of jamming I closed my eyes, and just as I was dozing off, I heard a soft tap on the window. Thinking it was a crackhead I angrily open my eyes, but upon realizing who it was, my cold stare quickly turned into fright. Peering into the car with a bright flashlight, I could see it wasn't a crackhead but the NYPD.

"Step out of the car now!" he barked. I got out of the car without hesitation and nervously closed the door. "Whose car is this?" the officer asked sternly.

"My pops," I responded back confidently. "He's upstairs, and I'm just waiting for him sir," I added. I could see the cop wasn't buying my line. He stared at me briefly, studying my posture and waiting for me to break character, but I didn't.

As soon as the cop looked like he was buying my story, Deondre appeared from out of the building.

"Yo nigga let's roll!" he yelled without realizing the cop standing there. When he did realize the situation, he froze on the last step. A huge, shit-eating grin covered the cops face.

"Come here you little fucker," he commanded. "You're both going to jail," he said scowling at us.

"Shit!" Deondre muttered. "Officer it's my car. He didn't have nothing to do with nothing," he told the cop. The officer gave me a once over then ordered me to go home. I told Deondre that I would tell his mom where he was being booked then bolted to the nearest train station.

The train ride seemed to last forever, but it was only thirty minutes. My blood was still rushing from the run-in with the cop, and my high was fading away like a shirt falling off. Once I got to my stop, I felt a jolt of fear rush through my entire body. As I exited the train, I saw what looked like ten Latin Squad boys.

"Fuck is up?" one of them barked as I passed to get off the train. Frozen in fear, I turned slowly to reply but as soon as I opened my mouth to speak, the doors quickly closed behind me.

"Maybe stealing the car was worth it," I thought as I walked through the turnstile. Deondre was right, fucking Latin Squad boys.

When I made it to Deondre's building I opened the graffiti-covered door, shuffling past a crackhead and sprinted up the steps.

Almost immediately upon approaching Deondre's unit, his mother opened the door.

"Where's Deondre'?" she asked urgently.

"The Bronx precinct," I flatly replied. She didn't even ask me the details, she just grabbed her jacket from the nearby coatrack and left. As I stood mute, I watched her stout body wobble down the hall thinking how worried she must be about Deondre. That thought must have lasted only a few seconds because I quickly began to worry about my own situation. What was I going to tell my mother? I knew I couldn't hide it from her, because she would eventually find out through Deondre's mother. That thought made me sweat even more. When I opened my door, I explained what happened then quickly darted to my room. Oddly enough, she didn't scold me. She just stayed in her room and softly told me goodnight.

The next day I found out Deondre was detained without bail. Two weeks later I learned he was sentenced to five years in a juvenile detention center. I was now without a friend.

Black Devil-Blue Eyes

Chapter Three
High School exit-college entrance

It was the summer of 2001. I just received my diploma and a full scholarship to Hudson University in upstate New York, one of the most prestigious colleges in the country. Once I was enrolled, I decided to take the finance and investment program. I paid attention, excelled in class, and even made the dean's list. Shit was nothing. See growing up, I always had this Pentium processor chip-like brain. Classwork, assignments, and projects were nothing.

The teachers took a liking to me because I showed promise and, per them, I was highly intelligent. The white teachers were impressed by me. I don't know, I guess because I was black and smart. Like that was a rarity? Don't get me wrong. I believe some white teachers genuinely liked me, but I could tell when smug fuckers were looking straight at me. You look into someone's eyes long enough; you begin to read people like a book. See, to me, most of what a person says is done with their eyes, not with their mouth. Anyways, while I was there, I was a fucking prodigy.

What I liked though were the parties. I always found time to have a good time. I went to all the parties; black parties and white parties. Anyone that says stupid shit like, "We're all the same," is a fucking idiot. See, growing up in the ghetto, I knew full well how my hood counterparts had fun. I practically could write a book about it with all the block parties I went to.

When it comes down to it, we *do* party a little different. Hanging with the white kids, was like a class in itself. They would get high and drunk and play beer pong or other games. One game they seemed to like a lot was, as I like to call it, 'ask the black guy questions.

They would ask shit like, "Why do black girls have attitudes?" or "Why do black guys have street names and use slang?" and "Are black guys as tough as they appear to be?" You'd be surprised to learn that white people, even drunk, are careful not to piss you off while asking their questions. I mean really? Drunk and you're still careful!? They'd also ask me questions like, "Why do you have green colored eyes and sandy brown hair?" Or, "why didn't I look like other black guys." I gingerly explained to them that my mother was biracial and my father was black, but strangely enough, they'd forget, and I'd end up explaining it again and again. Yeah, the parties are what I loved the most.

Like I said, I got a full scholarship with room and board, but I didn't have extra cash to do anything else. I had no car and no money, so I mostly did a lot of fucking. The white girls I dated would always wonder what color the baby would be if they had one. The black girls knew exactly what the baby would look like. "Fucking hilarious," I would always think. I lost a lot of girls though, because fucking gets old real fast, and I think I was too smart for them unless they were inebriated. I mean I wasn't a stiff or a lame but girls wanted to have fun. See girls like doing things, and they like going places so you can imagine how long a relationship with me lasted. I could have gotten a job, but I was devoted to school, and I didn't want any other matters hindering my studies. On the other hand, I was growing exhausted of never having any money.

Chapter Four
The day I met the devil

Then I met Conchita Carmelita Roseen. I was standing in the cafeteria line and I couldn't stop looking at her ass. She was the most beautiful woman I had ever seen.

"Were you just looking at my ass?" she frankly asked when she turned around. She must've had eyes in the back of her head. My jaw almost hit the ground in disbelief that she knew.

"I, I," is all I could manage to utter.

"It's okay," she said in a thick Latin accent. "I like your eyes, they're pretty," she continued. Seeing that she liked something about me, I sighed in relief. Then I quickly regained my composure and introduced myself.

"I'm George," I said.

"Nice name. I'm Conchita," she replied with a slight smile on her face. "Why are you smiling?" she then asked.

"Because *you're* smiling," I stupidly replied. I was usually smoother with women, but for some reason, this girl had me flustered. Standing about five feet three with the brownest complexion I had ever seen, I was in awe. Ironically enough, she complimented me on my eyes, but her's were even more beautiful; resembling that of a sky blue. While talking to her, I began to feel onlookers watching in anticipation of the next words that came out of my mouth, so we quickly ushered food onto our trays and headed for refuge. We talked for an hour about our families, where we were from, and our rocky adjustment to college life.

After realizing I was late for my first class, I quickly grabbed my books and scrambled out of the chow hall. The whole time in class, I couldn't seem to get her blue eyes out of my head. Not to mention, her round ass. It was like she was the prototype model for every beautiful woman. I couldn't wait for class to end so I could see her again. Dumbfounded by her beauty, I hadn't even asked her what dorm she stayed in.

After class, I entered the sea-like hallways hoping to catch a glimpse of her dark-brown complexion. Disappointed by not seeing her again, I robotically I wrote notes, recorded assignments, and jotted things down without paying attention to anything. As time floated by, I seemed to be distracted by thoughts of Conchita's beauty.

The next day I made sure I was in the chow hall at the same time. Impatiently waiting to see Conchita, I began making up lines in my head of what I'd say as soon as I saw her. Nine o'clock turned into ten o'clock and still no Conchita. Disappointed, I took a couple bites of my meal then discarded my food. Not seeing her killed my appetite. My first class was painful as hell as I couldn't stop thinking about Conchita. I wrote down notes on cue but couldn't entirely devote my attention to what the instructor was teaching.

While mindlessly sitting in my American History class, I decided to get some water to break the monotony going on inside my head. Upon exiting the class, I looked down the hall and noticed that I wasn't the only one taking a break. Out the corner of my eye, I saw Conchita entering the lady's restroom. "*Fucking finally*," I thought to myself. Wasting no time, I quickly made my way towards the lady's restroom, but by the time I got near, I became dumbfounded.

"*What was going to be my reason for being near the lady's room?*" I thought to myself. By the time I had devised a plan she was exiting and staring straight at me.

"Hola Papi, what are you doing? This is the ladies' room," she said smiling. So as not to come off like a bumbling idiot I put together the smoothest line I could think of.

"Well actually, I was getting something to drink. It just so happened that I saw you come out the restroom as soon as I was getting some water," I told her. "*Hah, I didn't sound like an idiot,*" I thought. She sized me up, quickly studying my body language for something to signal that I was lying.

"Okay so..., now you've found me, now what?" she said mockingly.

"I didn't think that far," I admittedly replied. I wasn't trying to game her, but I could see I was going to have to do a little more convincing.

"I like you, Papi. I don't know why but I do," she said sincerely. "Do you want to go back to my dorm room?" she continued.

"Yeah," I answered excitedly.

Once we got to her dorm room, she kissed me passionately. I instantly felt vibrations surge through my body like lightning. I kissed her back with every force of energy I had. While on campus I had my share of casual encounters but this felt different. She hungrily lifted my shirt over my head and began to kiss my chest aggressively. As she kissed me, I fumbled to pull her shirt from around her head. Taking charge, she pushed me back onto the bed and slung her top and bottoms off.

Then as I rushed to get naked she stopped me,

"Let me do it," she said. I obeyed. She quickly grabbed my warm-ups and slid them off with ease. Once she was completely naked, the sight of her was so beautiful I had to take it in and absorb it like a sponge. Her skin was the color of chestnuts with even darker nipples, making my mouth water. Her hair was jet black and was the texture of silk flowing over her narrow shoulders. As the fan in her room shifted cool air around, the breeze blew her hair making it look like a black water fountain.

Noticing that I could hardly contain myself, she leaped on top of me like a wild lioness. The different positions we swapped made me feel like that rabbit in that Bambi movie. The whole-time I was inside her I could feel her pulsating heart wrapped around my lower member. While her dorm room was filled with a slight breeze, we sweated against each other like fish slapping high waves.

"Oh Papi, Oh Papi, do it like that," she said every time my chest pressed against her chocolate nipples, and I thrusted into her pelvis. We made love for what seemed like hours, and with every movement, I could feel her perfume laced body get hotter and hotter. As I sucked her nipples, it seemed as if I were trying to put out flames that had spread across her body. Every time I thrusted into her, I felt my body reaching its peak. Unable to contain myself any longer, I erupted inside of her and then rolled onto my side.

"That was nice," she dizzily said. I felt the same way; only I couldn't seem to form a coherent sentence. She must've known that because she didn't even question the gibberish I had just said. She just rubbed my face and kissed my chest. Unable to keep my eyes open I dozed off into a euphoric-like state and went to sleep.

Dreams don't feel this good. Do they?

Chapter Five
The beginning of a good thing

The first time we went out on a date, she told me in her thick accent,

"No Papi, you save your couple of dollars." After that, the gesture was always sweet, but also embarrassing.

See, Conchita had received a full scholarship also, but her family had a couple of dollars so going to school and having fun was no problem for her. The whole time we dated I was slightly jealous of her. Even though she'd hit me off with some money when I needed, I would always think, *"Why couldn't my folks have had any money?"* But I liked her, so I wouldn't dwell on the idea for too long. I enjoyed her company, and every time we met up, it was like a new encounter. It never got boring. If we went to the movies, it was all paid for by her. If we went to dinner, she'd take care of the check. Nights at a play, she'd buy the tickets. Hell, if it were a town fair she'd buy the tickets *and* purchase the cotton candy. To her fun wasn't a problem. She stressed to me that it didn't matter about money. All that mattered to her was that I treat her right. So, I happily obliged. Not because she was sexy as hell, but because I didn't want to betray her kindness.

After a year had gone by, we were still wild about each other. We even decided to get an apartment off campus. The idea was mostly Conchita's, and her mother had even given her a check to pay for a year's worth of rent. I had some reservations at first, mostly because I didn't have a job, but Conchita told me not to worry; that she would be handling everything. The sex was still amazing, and my grades couldn't have been better. I was doing well. I had grown accustomed to being catered to like a king, and she liked my company. Our schedules also couldn't have meshed together any better. We'd wake up at 7 a.m., shower together, and then grab breakfast on our way to our eight o'clock class. We even arranged some of our classes on the same day. Things couldn't have been any better. We would spend all weekend together either doing homework or dining out.

One evening after making love, I noticed a hickey on my neck in the shape of a devil's head with horns.

"Baby, come look at this," I yelled.

"What? What do you want?" she shouted back irately. Sensing the irritation in her voice, I figured I wouldn't stress it.

"It's nothing. Don't worry about it," I replied. I guess she figured she wasn't going to let her favorite television show be distracted for no reason, so she got up from the chip ridden sofa and burst into the bathroom.

"What is it?" she sharply asked.

"See this shit?" I pointed to the purple color bruise on my neck. "You gotta stop leaving these where people can see em'. Shit, looks like a devil with horns. It's not a good look, especially if I want to be taken seriously as a professional," I told her. She attentively listened to me, then she mockingly replied,

"Oh Papi, lo siento, but I must leave my mark on everything that is mine." She knew it got on my last nerve when she called me Papi, but as beautiful as she was it was hard to stay mad at her. Especially, when she gave me the puppy dog eyes. I paused for a split second, then stared at her brown cheeks arched up, as she shot me a devilish smile. She was wearing her favorite boy shorts, and I couldn't help but google her coca cola shaped frame while she stood in the bathroom doorway.

"It's all good," I lazily said as she turned around and seductively walked back to the living room. Then returning my attention back to the mirror, I shook my head staring at the devil-shaped mark, took a deep breath, and swatted the light switch off. Upon exiting the bathroom, I stood momentarily in the hallway admiring her beauty from a distance. After moving in together, it was moments like this that made me smile the most.

As I stared at her from the hall, she slowly broke her attention away from the T.V. and looked at me.

"I love you," she mouthed as I blew her a kiss. Then I proceeded to the bedroom to study. Once I sat on the bed, I cracked open my textbook and began whisking through the pages, gorging the information. For me, studying was always a breeze and it never took long to retain information. After two hours into my studies, Conchita exploded into the room.

"*Papito!*" she yelled. "I want to go to Bruno's pub. Come on Papi, let's get a drink and some fajitas, she added."

"What happened when I was in the bathroom earlier? Not right now baby. You see me studying?" I replied.

For a moment, there was a brief pause,

"Well, I was watching my show but now it's off, and I'm hungry Papi," she whined.

"As much as I'd love too baby, you know I got to finish this paper by tomorrow," I said.

"Well... We can order the fajitas and get only one drink," she said putting her right hand down her shorts while touching her crotch. My attention quickly shifted from my studies, as my manhood grew watching her strip in the doorway.

"Damn baby, you really know how to distract me, don't you?" I said sarcastically. Slowly walking towards me totally naked, she replied,

"Yeah Papi, but you like it, don't you?" she said with an evil smile on her face. If I had said anything other than yes, I'd be lying. Then she jumped into my arms, straddling her legs around my waist while fumbling inside my gym shorts.

"You wanna do something really nasty when we get back?" she whispered in my ear.

How could I turn down a request like that? I slung the book I was holding onto the floor, palmed her other butt cheek, and violently kissed her juicy lips. Becoming hard as a rock, I proceeded to slide my manhood inside of her, when all of a sudden she hopped off my waist.

"Later! Come on; get dressed," she said. I hated when she left me high and dry, but the thought of what we were going to do later made me put my hard-on, on standby.

When we got to Bruno's the lights were dim, and people were standing wall to wall. Bruno's Pub was always crowded. There were people jam-packed at the bar, and every booth was occupied. The only free area was by the pool tables. While I loved to shoot pool, Conchita wanted to eat, and there weren't any chairs, only a beer spilled table.

"Miss," I said flagging down a server. "Could somebody wipe down this table and get some chairs? We're about to order some food, and I don't want to sit down in this mess," I quipped.

"Okay, gotcha," she replied energetically. The food and the chipper wait staff was what I liked the most about this place. No matter how much of a shit mood you seemed to be in, they were always nice to you. Conchita, I could tell, was in her regularly festive mood. Oblivious to my demeanor she bounced her body to the music pouring out of the surround-sound speakers in the pub.

"Hey Papi, I love the music they're playing. Too bad this isn't a nightclub or my ass would be all over the floor," she shouted. Before I could respond to her comment, the chipper little waitress trotted back up.

"Here you are," she said wiping the table. When she was done she then proceeded to take our order. "Okay, now what can I get you two fine folks?" she said trying to compete with the pub noise. Before the woman could finish her inquiry, Conchita started rolling out her order like a flooding river.

"I would like some fajitas, with extra cheese, Rum, and coke, make that two rum and cokes and can you bring me some chips and salsa with a lot of napkins?" I don't know if it was Conchita's thick accent, the speed in which she said it, or the competing noise in the pub, but when she was finished the waitress had a perplexed look on her face.

"Yeah…." she slowly said before adding, "Miss, I only got the fajitas and extra cheese. Can you tell me the rest again?" Having to repeat her order, I could tell Conchita was slightly agitated, but out of the kindness of her heart, she slowly and loudly did it anyways. Deciding I'd make the server's night a little easier, I simply ordered a Jack and coke.

After an hour and four drinks in, the night began to progress smoothly, but in the back of my mind my term paper was eating away at me.

"What's wrong Papi?" Conchita said as if she were reading my mind. I hesitated to answer her at first but eventually did.

"Nothing, I'm just thinking about my assignment is all," I said. Conchita had finished her fajitas a while ago, and we were into our fourth round of drinks, but she was never the one to be inconsiderate.

"Well we can go, honey, if you want. I don't want to keep you up all night," she replied. She flagged down the waitress, paid the check, and we hurried towards the exit.

As soon as we approached the door to leave, three biker guys walked in and blocked the doorway.

"Hey sexy, what's your name?" one of the guys said. Trying to avoid a confrontation we ignored them and walked outside of the pub. Feeling like we had dodged the bullshit, we both sighed in relief. However, the feeling was short lived when we stepped outside and were soon greeted by the same three bikers that were inside the pub.

"Hey girl, did you hear me or does your boyfriend gotcha' leash on too tight," said the fat aging one that must've been the leader.

"Look man, she's my girl. I don't want any problems, so could you just step the fuck off?" I barked.

"Man fuck you! What you going to do about it if I don't?" He angrily replied. Gauging the situation, I could tell this wasn't going to be easily resolved, so I initiated the first blow. Surprisingly enough, the punch I threw landed smack dab in the center of his face causing him to crash onto the pavement. As the adrenaline rushed through my body, I began to take a stance in preparation to brawl with the other two. To my surprise, they didn't even make a move towards me. They just picked their friend up off the ground and hurried back into the bar scolding him. When I turned around to see if Conchita was okay she was frozen in amazement.

"Wow Papi, you knocked him the fuck down," she said excitedly. "I ain't going to' lie, I thought he was going to kill you. He was big, but you know I would've had your back right?" she continued. Feeling at ease that she was okay, I begin to survey the damage to my right hand. "*No cuts*," I thought. It was surprising there wasn't any damage to my hand considering the guy's face felt like a brick wall, but despite the flawlessness of my hand it was throbbing like hell.

"Damn baby! My hand hurts like shit," I said in excruciating pain. As she rapidly looked over my hand the wind began blowing relentlessly. Wanting to escape the brutal cold Conchita and I decided to hurry down the avenue and back to our apartment.

Chapter Six
Day in-day out

It seemed like I had just gone to sleep when I was awakened by my annoying ass alarm clock. I hated getting up in the mornings. No matter how routine it was for me, I never could get used to it. The only thing I liked about it was pulling back the blankets and staring at Conchita's brown naked body.

Her back perfectly arched, even in her sleep, and round ass poking out as if she was motioning for me to slide into the crest of her ass. The sight always made me smile. After a quick glance at her, I jumped out of bed and pulled the blankets up to her shoulders. She usually got up moments later after I did, but this was one of her hangover days.

"Hey baby," I quietly said. "Wake up." She pulled the blanket over her head and whimpered,

"No Papi, I'm not going. You go. I don't feel like it." Because the sight of her hungover always made me smile, I respectfully obliged. After absorbing her beauty, I quickly raced into the bathroom. The shower felt like a heated underwater geyser causing the bathroom to fill up with steam. After a hot night of passionate love making, this was what my body needed. I felt totally relaxed. I could've stayed in the shower all day, but the thought of that assignment sharply dawned on me.

"Oh shit!" I said in a panic, after frantically shutting off the water and pulling back the shower curtain. I was feeling slightly nauseated from drinking last night, but the urgency of completing my assignment forced me into a blur. I scrambled for everything, making a mental checklist, so as not to forget anything behind. Once equipped and ready, I bolted out the door. I was so glad me and Conchita decided to get an apartment six blocks away from the university, as opposed to that swank place we looked at that was five miles away.

I made it to my first class, surprisingly, with fifteen minutes left to spare. Once inside the classroom, I broke out my laptop and all my important notes. Capitalizing on the extra minutes I had, I begin to feverishly type out the rest of my paper. By the time class had started, I had finished my paper, printed it out, proofread it, and made all the necessary changes.

The instructor never started class right on time however. He would always sip his coffee while cryptically watching us scramble to get our reports or assignments in order. It almost seemed as if he was watching us like his favorite television show. When I handed in my assignment his face shifted as if he were viewing a new episode from his regular program.

"Ahh mister Sphinx, looks good," he said while quickly scanning the cover sheet. Every time I handed in a paper, it was always a new response.

"Yeah, I hope. I put everything into that assignment," I said as if on cue.

"You always do mister Sphinx. You always do," he said with a gentle smile on his face. I took in his admiration then coolly returned to my seat. Then as the instructor began to warm up his lecture, my hangover had crept up on me like an enormous, 600-pound gorilla. The feelings of nausea, a pulsating headache, and cold sweat began setting in. So as not to disturb the class, I stealthily made my exit to the lavatory.

Ten minutes later, after spewing my out guts, I returned to class to find the instructor on a topic that I wasn't entirely knowledgeable of. Realizing this, I quickly hurried to my desk and began writing notes.

After class, I gathered my things and began heading to my next class, when all of a sudden, I was stopped by a beautiful blonde woman.

"Hi," she said energetically. I was feeling like shit, but the sight of this woman drowned out any ill feelings I may have been experiencing and was replaced with intrigue.

"Hey... uh, can I help you? I curiously ask.
"Oh, sorry about that, my name is Judica Roetta. I noticed that you always seem to get very high scores on your papers. I was wondering if maybe we could study together sometime," she asked.

"Sure," I aptly replied.

"Okay, I'll give you my number, and you can give me yours, and we'll hook up every Wednesday to study," she said as her blue eyes beamed like a crystal ball. We exchanged numbers, and as she walked away, I could sense some chemistry between her and I. The thought might've been wrong, but as she walked away, I couldn't help but notice her round petite ass. After surveying her frame, I suddenly realized that my next class was about to start. Alarmed, I darted out of the classroom and quickly made my way to the Carver Hall.

Three classes in and I was feeling like a sundried turd. The feeling was subsided when I felt my phone vibrate, and I checked to see who was calling. It was Conchita. Finally, she had woken up.

"Hello," I smoothly answered.

"Hey, Papi, how's your day going?" She asked softly.

"It's going okay, I almost threw up my guts earlier, but I'm fine now. Thanks for asking," I said. I could tell from the sound of her voice that she was still lying down, and chances are, she hadn't even gotten out of the bed.

"Well, I didn't want anything, I just called to hear your voice," she said. That made me smile.

"I was gonna call you earlier, but I didn't want to disturb you. I know you probably have a crazy headache, huh?" I replied.

"I did, but I took some Excedrin that you had on the nightstand. Well baby, call me later. I'm going back to bed," she softly said.

"Bye baby," I replied. After hanging up the phone, I studied the call list for a brief second then raced to my next class.

The day almost seemed to blur past as I slid my key into the front door. As soon as I entered the apartment, I walked straight to the bedroom to check on Conchita.

"Hey Mami," I softly said as I studied her silhouette through the blanket. She slowly rolled over and opened her eyes like a newborn baby.

"Hey Papi," she whispered. Why didn't you call me later?" she inquired.

"I started to, but I figured I'd let you get your rest," I told her.

"It's okay; I know you were busy with classes today," she replied. I stood in the doorway observing her juicy lips and disheveled hair, and as she spoke, the only thing I could think is that this must be the most agreeable woman I had ever been in a relationship with. Then in a childlike voice, she requested for me to get her some orange juice from the store. To which I happily obliged, tossing my stuff down onto the bed and hurrying back out of the apartment.

The walk to the neighborhood market seemed to take forever, and as I approached the entrance, I let out a sigh of relief. Once inside, I scanned the aisles to quickly locate the orange juice.

I hadn't decompressed since I left school, so I wanted to spend the least amount of time walking around the store as possible. When I found it, I swiped the juice out the freezer and raced for the checkout booth. As soon as I turned around, I was greeted by Judica.

"Hey... Uhh Judica," I said in disbelief. "What are you doing here?

"You can call me Judi," she replied goofily. "I live around here, what are you doing here?" she continued.

"I live around here also," I replied.

"Cool, well since we live near one another can we study at your place?" she politely asked.

"Uhh, I don't think that's a good idea," I reluctantly answered.

"Why? You gotta girlfriend? That's okay; we can study at my place. I don't want you to get into any trouble," she said with a smirk on her face.

"I think that's best," I said flatly.

"Cool, well, I'll see you in class tomorrow. Bye-Bye Georgie," she said seductively as she turned to walk away. This time she waltzed off a little sexier as if she knew I was staring at her ass.

So once again, I stood in place statuesque-like, staring at her for longer then I should have. Then I quickly purchased the juice and darted back to the apartment.

Upon entering the front door, I could see Conchita had managed to slither out of bed and was up and about.

"Hey, baby I got Tropicana. I hope that's alright. It was all they had," I said, but as I waited for a reply, I could tell something had changed in her mood. I observed her demeanor for a moment and could tell she was pissed off but dismissed the thought as I went to put the orange juice in the fridge. As I walked to the kitchen I could sense Conchita following me. When I turned around, she was standing right behind me visibly angry.

"Baby what's the matter?" I innocently asked.

"You don't know?" she shot back. Never being the one to argue I asked again,

"What's the matter?"

"Some puta named Judica called your phone! She left a text message that said, 'By the way, I like your eyes.' I talked to you earlier, and you didn't mention no bitch! What the fuck Papi!" She said with rage in her voice.

"Baby calm down and let me explain. I met her in one of my classes today. She wanted to study with me since that paper I handed in last week got me an A. That's all. You seemed very tired when I talked to you, and it slipped my mind is all. I'm sorry," I said reassuringly.

"Papi you not fuckin' around with that bitch, are you? Because you know I will cut your dick off," she said harshly.

"I promise I'm not fuckin' around with her, I don't think she likes me anyway," I said.

"You better not be mother-fucker," she said sharply.

"Why I gotta be a mother-fucker?" I jokingly replied.

"Because you are fuckin' me, and I'm Mami, motherfucker!" She said as she burst into laughter. "Anyways, since we cleared that shit up, I must say I am feeling better, but you know what I could really use?" she quizzed.

"Some dick?" I fired back.

"Yeah, how'd you know?" she knowingly asked.

"Because I need some pussy," I answered back laughing hysterically. She then casually reached into my pants and proceeded to stroke my member. With one arm, I scooped her naked body off the floor and carried her into the room. Once we were on the bed I wasted no time piercing her tight, wet opening as she kissed my chest ferociously.

Black Devil-Blue Eyes

Chapter Seven

How things unravel

The following Wednesday had come faster than I expected, and Judi was calling like clockwork.

"Hello," I innocently answered.

"Hey are you still on campus?" the voice on the other end asked.

"Yeah, I am," I replied.

"Well, change of plans," she said. "I can't study in the school library. Is it alright if you come over here? It's a little quieter," she continued.

"*If I went to another woman's house what would Conchita think?*" I asked myself. I tried to reason in my head that it was only studying and nothing more. "*What's the worst that could happen?*" I continued. Just the thought was making me nervous, but I reluctantly obliged, got directions to her apartment building, and hung up the phone.

As I sat on the garbage ridden bus, my cell phone began to ring violently. It was Conchita. With great reservation, I answered the phone.

"Hey Mami," I said trying to conceal my guilt.

"Hey Papi, is something wrong?" she questioned.

"Naw, everything's fine. I'm just on the bus going to the Justine Hall to study, that's all," I explained.

"When is your last class again?" she asked.

"Three o'clock," I answered back.

"Good, well when you get done meet me at Bruno's. Let's celebrate; I got an 'A' on my quiz. I could use a drink to take the edge off," she said.

"Alright baby, I'm down with that," I replied. After hanging up the phone, I stared at the screen. The longer I stared at the phone; the guiltier I felt. Suddenly, the bus hit a pothole and I realized my stop was quickly approaching.

I rung the bell, and when the bus stopped, I casually exited. Judi had given me the apartment address, so it was easy navigating through the maze courtyard to her unit. It was funny though, Judi lived on the same side of town as me, and for some reason the scenery seemed cleaner. There were flowers planted everywhere, and you could even hear the birds chirping.

Once I got to her doorstep, I rang the bell. Expecting to see the same conservative girl from class, to my surprise, who answered the door was not the same woman. The girl from class had glasses and dirty blonde hair. *This* girl was wearing contacts and had freshly dyed bright blonde hair. She even managed to shed the reserved clothing for a tight-fitting tank top and Pink boy shorts. "*I never understood why they were called boy shorts. I never saw any guys wear those shorts,*" I thought.

"Well come on in," she said as she ushered me into her small spaced studio. "I made some fajitas and rice if you're hungry," she said with a devious smile on her face. I hadn't eaten all day, but the aroma was enough to make you hungry even if you *did* just eat. As my stomach growled, I took a seat on the frumpy faded blue loveseat and began opening my book bag. While rummaging through my bag, I looked up and couldn't help but stare right at Judy's little round ass as she bent over to retrieve the tortillas from the oven.

I don't know if it was the aroma emitting from the tortillas or the sight of her shorts riding up her ass that made my mouth salivate. After a few seconds of staring, I quickly turned my attention back to my bag.

"Hey, we got time for that. Here's your food," she said as she lowered a plate onto the living room table.

"Damn, it tastes as good as it smells," I said as I shoveled a fajita into my mouth. Ironically, Conchita liked to cook fajitas too, and even though her food was good, it didn't taste this delicious. As I continued chewing, I began feeling extremely guilty.

"So, you like?" she asked as if my loud chewing wasn't confirmation enough.

"This is the best thing I've eaten all day," I answered back shoveling beans into my already full mouth.

"Good, good. Well, I got some sodas if you would like one," she said as she abruptly popped up from the loveseat. I noticed the whole time I was cramming my face, that she wasn't eating anything.

"Hey, aren't you gonna fix yourself a plate?" I asked curiously.

"I ate before you came over. I figured I'd offer you some when you got here," she calmly replied.

"You're so sweet. Thanks for thinking of me," I jokingly said.

"Now, do you want a strawberry or grape soda?" she asked sweetly.

"Grape" I replied, continuing to shove beans and rice into my face.

"So, does your girl cook?" she asked with a slight smirk on her face.

"Yeah she does," I answered back solemnly.

"How long have you been with her?" she curiously asked. At that moment I knew Judi was up to something, but I pretended to be naïve and played along.

"A little over a year now," I answered back.

"That's good. I'm glad to see there are still some loyal guys out there," she retorted. We talked for an hour about our views on relationships, but after a while I began to think of Conchita and the fact that she probably thought I was still at school.

"Hey, I don't mean to be rude, but you want to start studying?" I abruptly asked.

"Sure. Yeah, let's do that. I get carried away sometimes," she said. After a few hours of studying, I began to grow tired and was longing to stretch out.

"Hey, it's getting late, I gotta go. My girl is gonna wonder where I'm at," I nervously said.

"Oh, I understand she said with a devious grin on her face. Before I left, I offered to help with the dishes, but she generously declined. She insisted that it wouldn't be hospitable to allow a guest to clean up after a meal. So, I gathered my things, left the tiny apartment, and headed to the bus stop.

When I got outside, while fumbling for my bus schedule, a gush of wind suddenly blew past me. I had been at Judi's apartment for almost five hours and didn't expect it to be so cold.

"Why didn't I bring a heavier coat?" I thought as I quickly zipped up my jacket. As I waited on the bus, suddenly my phone rang.

"Where the fuck are you?" The voice on the other end screamed.

It was Conchita.

"Hey, hey, chill out!" I sternly said but she wasn't having it, and I could tell that my calm demeanor only further enraged her.

"No motherfucker, you said you were gonna' study for a few hours at the Justine Hall!" she shouted.

"So, what?" I responded.

"So, what? What the fuck you mean, so what? After a few hours went by I got curious and I went there, and guess what? You weren't there mother fucker!" she said angrily. "You didn't even bother calling either, so what the fuck huh?" she continued. I was stumped. I had nothing. No comeback at all. Funny thing is though; I didn't do anything wrong with Judi, but my situation was looking very condemning.

"Okay, can we continue this conversation when I get home?" I quietly pleaded. There was silence over the phone for a few seconds before she replied,

"I'll see you when you get here motherfucker!" and then she hung up.

When I got back to the apartment, I expected to see Conchita in the narrow hallway ready to give me a verbal lashing, but she was nowhere in sight. The lights were off, and the apartment was pitch-black. I checked all the rooms and still no Conchita. I begin to grow worried. She had never done this before, so I was completely perplexed at her mysterious absence. She did say before she hung up on me, that she would see me when I got home, so I begin to calm down. *"Maybe she went to Bruno's Pub to blow off some steam,"* I thought.

Dismissing the idea that she would leave me for good, I tossed my things onto the floor and quickly began rummaging through the fridge in search of the Jack Daniels. When I opened the door and looked inside, I didn't see the bottle. Then the thought occurred to me that we had two bottles of Rum in the cabinet. As I poured myself a drink my mind began reverting to its original thought. *"Where did she go?"* Figuring I'd give her a call, I raced back to where I had tossed my jacket and quickly retrieved my cell phone. Frantically, I begin to dial. The phone rang, what seemed like twenty times, before going to voicemail. I tried several more times but got the same result. By the fifth try, I started growing angry. Feeling my blood boil, I calmly placed the phone back in my pocket and returned to the kitchen to continue my drink.

After a few hours of mindless television, I began growing exhausted waiting for Conchita to arrive, so I turned the TV off and stumbled drunkenly towards the bedroom. When I entered the room, I flopped onto the bed like a dead fish and blacked out into oblivion.

Chapter Eight
The devil's dog

The following morning, I was awakened by the smell of smoked bacon, and French toast. As I surveyed the room, I looked under the blanket and noticed I was completely naked. Conchita must've come home while I was asleep and undressed me. The threat she made days earlier about cutting my dick off had entered my mind, and for a brief second, I felt panic run through my entire body. I quickly looked under the covers and grabbed my penis tightly for reassurance.

"Still there," I said with a sigh of relief. Then I immediately sprang out of bed to find her. As I roamed the hallway, the aroma from the breakfast she was cooking seemed to emit stronger and stronger the closer I got. When I reached the kitchen, she was naked and battering some eggs.

"Hola Papi. I was wondering when you were gonna wake up. It's noon. What did you do? Drink yourself to sleep? Aww poor Papi. You should not do that," she said continuing to stir the bowl of eggs. "I was mad at you at first, but then I called Rita, and she said I should hear you out first. So, we went out, had some drinks and played darts. So, now that you're here and I'm here, can you explain to me where you were and how come you lied?" she continued.

"Okay, first off, Judi is in my class," I slurred before being interrupted.

"I know that motherfucker," she quipped.

"Okay," I continued, "Judi just wanted to study at her place because the hall was too noisy. I know I should've told you baby, but I forgot. Nothing happened, it was just a change of plans, and I should've told you, but I didn't. I'm sorry," I sincerely said. She stared at me for a brief while, then looked down at the bowl of eggs,

"You know I could've chopped your dick off, right? I'm going to tell you one last time... Stop pissing me off. You're starting to make me crazy. I love you Papi, and I don't wanna hurt you, but I will," she replied. As she slowly looked up at me, she shot me the coldest stare I had ever seen before. Her eyes were ice blue, and they sent fear through my entire body. After our brief conversation, she made me a huge plate which I began devouring once I sat down.

As the morning set in, it seemed as if the day was dragging along. When two in the afternoon came around, I still hadn't taken a shower or brushed my teeth. While sitting in a daze, my phone began to ring relentlessly. I picked it up, and the voice on the other end was none other than Judi.

"Uh, hi," I mumbled, still thinking about what Conchita had said earlier.

"Hey, I just wanted to say thank you so much for yesterday. I think I'm going to ace this class thanks to you," she said.

"Yeah, I think next time we better study at the library," I lazily told her. "My girl was mad as fuck." There was a brief silence, before she replied,

"You didn't tell her?" she asked.

"It slipped my mind and when she went to the Justine Hall and didn't see me, she started to freak out," I told her.

"Oh, I'm sorry; I didn't mean to get you into trouble. Alright, next week we'll study at the library. Problem solved," she said casually. I could tell that her response was contrived and not sincere at all.

"Since we got that out the way," she continued, "I was wondering if you were free Saturday. I'm throwing a party, and I invited a few friends. I thought you'd like to swing by. You can bring your girl too, so we could show her that there's nothing going on between us."

"Yeah, that'd be cool, I'll just hit you up in the daytime to let you know if I'm coming," I told her.

"That'll work," she replied. Then we both said our goodbyes and hung up. Moments later, as I was hanging up, Conchita entered the apartment.

"Who were you talking too?" she asked as she made her way to the living room.

"That was Judi from school. She wanted to know if I, I mean, if we'd like to come to her get-together Saturday night," I smoothly replied.

"You talking a whole lot to this puta lately aren't you Papi?" she said in her thick accent, "I don't wanna hang out with any puta that's texting my man saying he's got pretty eyes. What does she think I am? A dumb ass puta?" she asked rhetorically. As she ranted, I got up from the recliner, attempting to calm her down, I pulled her close to my chest and said,

"Mami trust me when I say, nothing is going on between her and I. She's just a classmate that I study with. Anyways, inviting you was her idea. Now come on, if something *was* going on do you think she would've asked for you to come?" I said pointedly. As soon as I said that, she pulled away from me and stared me down.

"She might be a sneaky bitch. I don't know her... Papi, you got to watch these sneaky puta's," she replied. Now the thought *had* occurred to me that Judi might've been up to something but I quickly dismissed it as a friendly invitation. After our brief spat, Conchita's mood began to lighten up.

"Hey, guess what I got while I was out?" she trivially asked. As I vigorously tried to guess, she broke away from my grasp and darted into the kitchen and out the front door. As I stood in the middle of the living room, my mood shifted to utter disappointment when she returned and presented me with her newfound find.

"A dog?" I said. And not just any dog, but a Shih Tzu. The fact that she knew I hated dogs made me believe she went out and bought it purely out of spite. At the mere sight of the dog, I became incensed.

"I'm not cleaning up any shit! The minute it starts to shit all over the place you're the one responsible for cleaning it up," I barked while she did her little joyous dance. She could tell I was mad, and the sight of my dismay only made her gyrate more.

"Yes Papi, I will clean up all the shit and feed him every day," she said in a condescending matter. "Now I have two dogs," she added with an enormous smile on her face.

As she bent over to pick up the dog, the sight of her shorts wedged between her cheeks made my manhood grow instantly.

"Hey, put him up, and let's go in the room," I whispered in her ear as I proceeded to grind on her.

"Oh, I go buy a dog, and now you want me doggy style?" she said nastily. Let's go," she continued as she bent over once more to set the dog down. As we raced to the bedroom, she began stripping in the hallway flinging her tank top and then her shorts. Once in the room, she leaped onto the bed face first, spreading her legs apart with her back arched up. At the very sight of her heart-shaped ass, I pounced on top of her like a wild lion. Still slightly hungover, I slid into the wrong hole causing her to squirm like a wriggling fish.

"No Papi that's the wrong hole," she said with discomfort. "If you're going to do that, get the lube," she added. After savagely making love we flounced onto the bed exhausted and sweaty.

Later that evening I awakened to the sound of the dog barking in the next room.

"What the fuck?" I shouted as I raced to see why the dog was barking like a maniac. Upon entering the living room, I discovered two enormous men sitting on the sofa talking to Conchita.

"What the fuck is the matter with the dog? And who the fuck are they?" I sternly asked.

"I'm Conchita's cousin, Roberto. You must be her boyfriend. It's okay, we heard a lot about you. My cousin seems to like you a lot," he said as he began to laugh. I looked over at Conchita with a sigh of relief waiting for an explanation.

"It's true Papi, he's my cousin. They just came into town, and they were looking for my brother Ralph. They couldn't find him, so mama told them to find me. I've been calling him, but he's not picking up," she said with alarm in her voice.

"Well, they couldn't have called you first? No offense fellas, but I wake up to find two big mother fucka's in the living room and the damn dog barking like a maniac. I mean what the fuck?" I said.

"Hey, take it easy. We didn't mean to startle you. We just needed to see our little cousin because we were worried about her brother," Roberto replied. After looking Roberto over for a moment, I calmed down, bummed a cigarette from him, and sat on the sofa next to Conchita.

"So, where do you guys think he could've gone? I mean, it ain't like someone wanted him dead, right? As soon as I said that, everyone in the living room just stared at me. I could tell from that comment that no one was feeling what I had just said and there was an uncomfortable silence beginning to settle in the room. Not wanting to feel awkward, I quickly changed the topic.

"Hey, does anyone want anything to drink?" I nervously asked. Everyone in the room nodded in agreement, and I quickly went to retrieve the bottle of Stolis' from the cupboard. While in the kitchen, I heard someone's mobile phone ring. Unable to make out the conversation, I continued fumbling with the glasses and the bottle of Stolis'. Upon my return, everyone's mood seemed to have shifted even more somber.

"What happened? Why is everybody looking so sad?" I said in sheer ignorance. I looked over at Conchita and could tell something horrible had happened. She was sobbing uncontrollably with her head buried in the unknown cousin's shoulder.

"What happened?" I asked again, this time with more emphasis.

"Her Madre just called. Ralph is in the hospital. He was hit by a, they think, a drunk driver. He's not dead, but he's in bad shape. They don't know if he's gonna make it," Roberto explained.

As I sat in the living room trying to grasp the entire situation, all I could focus on was Conchita crying like a baby.

"Mami, it's gonna be alright," I assured her as I rubbed her back.

After a few minutes of crying, she emerged from her cousin's shoulder with bloodshot eyes and said,

"Thank you, baby, you're so sweet. You know what; I'm going to go to my mother's house so I'll be close to the hospital in the morning. I'll be back around three, is that okay?" she softly asked. Analyzing the situation, I quickly gave my approval.

"It's cool baby. I understand," I nonchalantly said. Then she wiped her tear-stained face, straightened her hair, and quickly went into the bedroom to retrieve a few things for her overnight stay. After scrambling, she raced back into the living-room, kissed me on the cheek, and was out the door with her two gigantic cousins following in tow. As I sat on the sofa, I could still feel her moist kiss on my face. All of a sudden, I felt loneliness overcome me. Not having anything else to do, I casually gathered the glasses and bottle and dropped them off into the kitchen. Afterwards, I retreated to the bedroom and nestled under the blankets to get some much-needed sleep.

Black Devil-Blue Eyes

52

Chapter Nine
Deviating from the devil

The night seemed to have come and gone almost as soon as I closed my eyes. Having forgotten about Conchita's family situation, I awoke with anticipation of her lying beside me. When I looked over, I was confronted with the stark reality that she was gone. Knowing that she only went to her mother's house and would eventually return, put my anxiety at ease. The need to hear her voice forced me to call her cell. The phone rang on the other end for several seconds but then went to voicemail. I tried calling it again, but I got the same result. After several attempts my frustration began to grow and I hung up. Sitting motionless in the middle of the bed, I became enraged when suddenly my cell rang.

"Hello," I eagerly answered. After realizing the voice on the other end wasn't Conchita, my mood shifted from excited to somber. I think Judi sensed my frustration.

"What's eating you?" she asked.

"Nothing's wrong," I quipped.

"Oh, my bad, I see I've caught you at a bad time," she retorted.

"Sorry. I didn't mean to snap at you. It's just my girl's brother is in the hospital. She went to see him and I tried calling her, but she's not answering her phone," I said.

"Well, don't let that get you down. Maybe she's preoccupied. It *is* her brother. C'mon, have some patience," she said calmly. "If you don't mind me asking, what happened to him?" she added.

"He got hit by a car," I said coldly.

"Damn, that's serious. C'mon, don't you think you're being just a little bit selfish?" she asked rhetorically.

There was a brief silence over the phone, before I replied, "You're right," I said.

"Well, if you're not busy, wanna go see a movie with me? Just as friends," she slyly asked.

"Yeah, why not?" I casually responded. "Just let me freshen up, and I'll meet you at Dutch plaza like around two-thirty," I added.

"That's perfect. I'm already near Vegas Avenue at Jefferson Square Plaza window shopping," she said giggling. Hearing her giggle brought a smile to my face, and for a brief second, I had forgotten about Conchita not answering her phone. We said our farewells, and as soon as I hung up, I sprang out of bed like a wild leopard.

After what seemed like an hour-long shower, I quickly scrambled to find something to throw on. It must've been subconscious because when I looked into the mirror, it seemed as if I meticulously ironed my clothes. Something I only did for Conchita's satisfaction.

As I surveyed my appearance again, a slight feeling of guilt came over me. "*What reason do I have to feel guilty*?" I thought as I continued putting on my shoes. Once I was completely dressed, I studied my appearance in the mirror once more. Feeling fully satisfied with my attire, I quickly turned off the lights and raced out the front door. As I was walking to the nearest bus stop my cell phone rang. Hoping to hear Conchita's voice, I looked down at my cell and realized it was Judi again.

"Yeah," I solemnly answered.

"Hey, how close are you?" she asked.

"The bus comes in seven minutes. It should take me about fourteen minutes to get to you," I replied.

"Good, just checking. I was trying on some lingerie, and I kind of get carried away. Didn't wanna set my phone down and miss your call. Like I said, sometimes when I'm trying on stuff I get carried away and lose track of time," she said laughing.

"Cool, well if I call and you don't answer; I'll just meet you at... Wait, what's the place you're at? I asked in mid-sentence.

"V Secret silly," she replied.

"Cool. I'll hit you up when I get there," I said before hanging up. As soon as I ended the call with Judi, my cell phone rang again. Without checking the caller ID, I foolishly answered thinking it was Judi calling back.

"Hey Judi, what's up?" I said eagerly. As soon as I answered, I quickly realized it wasn't Judi at all.

"What the fuck! Judi? Why do you think it's that bitch?" The voice on the other end barked. It was Conchita.

"Hey baby, no, I thought it was her because she called earlier for clip notes is all. I didn't look at the caller ID, and I didn't think it was you calling, because I called you earlier and you didn't answer. Your phone just kept going to voicemail. My bad baby," I said as I coolly explained myself.

"Oh, well look at your caller ID, I don't like calling my man, and he thinks it's another bitch calling him," she replied. Then she added, "I'm going to come to the house and get some more clothes. My mother's a wreck, so I'm going to stay with her for a couple of weeks. Just until my brother's condition improves. Are you ok with that?"

"Yeah, its cool baby," I somberly answered. Sensing a slight change in my tone, she quickly inquired,

"What's wrong?"

"Nothing baby, I'm cool," I told her.

"Okay, well I'll see you when I get home," she quickly replied. As soon as I began telling her that I wouldn't be there, she hung up. I started to call her back, but I changed my mind as soon as the bus pulled up.

The bus ride to Jefferson Square was the longest ride I had ever taken. It wasn't that the trip took long, it just seemed like whoever oversaw the transit system somehow put the slowest drivers on the route. They drove like two miles an hour. Today the ride was even more excruciating. The paranoia of meeting up with Judi, while Conchita was worrying about her brother's health, coupled with the fact that the bus driver was stretching out a fourteen-minute ride was beginning to drive me up a wall. I was sweating like a person that had just robbed a bank. As soon as I wiped my sweat covered brow, I looked up, and I was at my stop. Glad to have finally arrived, I yanked the bell and quickly exited the bus.

As I made my way towards the plaza, I began to feel a slight breeze. I turned up my collar, looked around the square parking lot, and surveyed the area. The paranoia was mounting so much that I began to feel like James Bond on a mission. I knew Conchita was on the other side of town at the hospital, however, for some reason I felt like she was going to pop out from behind a parked car and catch me with Judi.

"I'm tripping," I thought to myself. *"It's just a movie,"* I continued to rationalize. As I walked behind a parked Cadillac, and up to the sidewalk of the theater, Judi surprised me from behind.

"Rah!" she screamed as she jumped onto my back. Shocked as hell, I spazzed,

"Judi what the fuck?! Don't do that shit!" I yelled. She quickly hopped off my back and regrettably looked down.

"I'm sorry. I didn't mean to scare you," she said.

"Nah, you didn't scare me, it's just that I didn't tell Conchita about this and I'm kinda nervous is all," I replied.

"Why didn't you tell her?" she sweetly asked. For a second, I almost thought she was serious, and then I remembered that this was the same girl frolicking around her apartment in booty shorts.

"Yeah right, whatever," I said as I looked at her skeptically.

Then she giggled at me as she grabbed my hand and we began walking towards the entrance of the theater. Once we were inside the lobby, Judi slipped her grip from around my arm.

"So...... What do you wanna see?" she kindly asked.

"Anything, it doesn't matter to me," I nonchalantly replied.

"Yes! I've been wanting to see that new Sandra Bullock movie!" she said excitedly. "You're too kind," she continued as she kissed me on the cheek and began rifling through her handbag. We quickly made it to the concession stand for treats, when suddenly my cell phone began to ring.

"Hello," I cautiously answered while walking away from Judi.

"Hello? Where are you mother fucker?" Conchita barked.

"I was trying to tell you earlier that I was going to catch a movie later, but you hung up on me," I calmly responded.

"Oh, uh, well when you gonna be back", she aggressively asked.

"Around six or so," I answered. "By the way, how is your brother doing?" I asked trying to change the subject.

"He has a fractured leg, two broken arms, a punctured lung, crushed pelvis, and a ruptured kidney. Doctors don't know if he'll make it, but they're doing everything they can. He's on a breathing machine right now, but I guess we'll just have to wait and see," she answered as her voice began to weaken.

"Well, baby it'll be alright. God's gonna take care of everything," I said trying to console her.

"Thank you Papi. I needed that," she said choking back tears. "Well, go see your movie and call me when you get out, okay? I'll probably be at my mother's house," she continued.

"Okay baby," I said as I blew a kiss into the phone. She blew me a kiss back, and then quickly hung up. After putting my phone back into my pocket, I briefly paused as the feeling of guilt began to set in. Feeling low, I kept telling myself, *"It's just a movie, nothing more."* Deciding not to dwell on the idea, I turned around to accompany Judi at the concession stand, but to my surprise, she was standing right behind me.

"How long have you been standing there?" I curiously asked.

"I just walked up," she said smiling like the Cheshire cat. Something in my gut told me that was a lie, but I casually dismissed the thought, and we began to make our way to the movie auditorium.

"Number eight. C'mon," she said grabbing my arm.
 Once inside, we surveyed the room, scouting what section to sit in as Judi led the way.

"How about the top," she said whispering in my ear.

"Cool, I don't care," I replied as the trailers began to louden. We sat down at the very top near the projector, and almost immediately, Judi began to ambush the bucket of popcorn.

"Goddamn! Slow down!" I barked.

"Sorry, but I'm hungry as shit. I haven't eaten all day," she said, still shoveling popcorn into her mouth.

Not long after she began gulping the soda down like a hungry traveler. After her hunger ceased, I was able to focus on the movie but couldn't help but inhale her perfume. It was unlike Conchita's. Conchita's perfume was strong and erotic, sort of like her demeanor. This was different. Judi's scent was softer, and just like her personality, was very elusive. It snuck up on me, catching me off guard until it overwhelmed me.

As Judi attentively watched the movie, I couldn't help but look at her periodically and study her innocent-like expressions. I knew she was up to something, but I was perplexed about her exact intentions. Did she want sex? Did she want to be in a relationship with me or both? Either way, I wasn't gonna make the first move. I was going to play along and see what angle she decided to use.

About an hour into the film, my thoughts were confirmed.

"I like your company. I know you have a girlfriend, but I'm not looking to get serious or nothing like that. I just like your company is all," she said whispering into my ear. As I intensely focused on her and the movie, I almost choked on my soda at what soon followed.

"Can I suck your dick?" she seductively asked. The request left no room for dialogue. I quickly juggled the thoughts around in my head like Houdini with a set of bowling pins. *"What about Conchita?"* I thought. *"It's only head,"* I continued to reason as she rubbed her hand slyly across the crotch part of my jeans. As the stimulation set in and my manhood grew, I started to give way to my animal instincts.

"Okay, yeah alright," I said as I unzipped my pants. The stroking of her hand amazed even me at the size of my massive hard-on.

"Damn it's thick!" she said in amazement. After placing the half-eaten bucket of popcorn on the floor, she proceeded to lower her face onto my lap. I hadn't noticed how cool it was in the theater room until I felt the heat inside the moist canal of Judi's mouth. She didn't even rush. Unlike Conchita, Judi didn't go up and down mechanically. She did tricks with her tongue. She sucked on the head like there was poison inside that she was trying to extract. As I stretched out and enjoyed the moment, I forgot I was holding onto the soda, and as the warm fuzzy feeling set in, I dropped it onto the floor. The suction of Judi's mouth engulfed me, and I didn't even care about the soda. When the feeling became too much for me, and I couldn't fight back the urge, I erupted into her mouth. She didn't even stop. She just kept sucking and swallowing simultaneously. The climax was extraordinary, but the ticklish feeling was beginning to implant itself into my dick, and I couldn't help but retrieve my member back into my jeans.

"Okay, okay" I muffled as I zipped up my pants.

"Keep this between us," she whispered as she turned her attention back to the movie. I was in momentary bliss and just as I was beginning to enjoy the feeling, my cell phone rang. Clearing my voice, I hesitantly answered the phone.

"Hello," I said.

"Baby, you still in the movie?" the soft voice asked.

"Yeah baby, it's almost over," I replied.

"Okay, I'm at the house. Mama said she was cool, so I came home because I miss you, baby. I need you, Papi," she girlishly said. The sound of her voice hit me like a ton of bricks. What had I done? I began to feel like shit. *"Fuck!"* I thought to myself. Hearing her in so much pain made me feel like the lowest of the lows.

"As soon as the movie ends I'm coming home," I told her.

"Okay Papi, I'll be up. Hurry," she softly said. When I hung up the phone, I began to feel heartbroken. The movie soon ended and the credits began to roll, as Judi and I regained our composer.

I adjusted my belt, brushed the remnants of popcorn from my lap, and made my way to the auditorium exit. When we got outside, Judi turned to me and proposed an idea,

"We can continue the tutoring; but, if you wanna fool around that's fine too," she said with a devilish expression on her face. "Well I'm parked over here," she continued as she pointed at the vacant parking lot. "You want a ride?" she curiously asked.

"Naw, I'm good. I'll just jump on the bus, it's not that far, but thanks though," I said apprehensively. Judi skeptically looked me up and down, as if seeing straight through my reason for denying her request. She bit her lower lip, gave me a wink, then turned around, and headed for her car. Before traveling in the opposite direction, I paused to stare at her curvaceous hips sway back and forth.

Once I got to the bus stop, the night wind began to blow harshly. For a split second, I almost regretted turning down Judi's request to drive me home. Standing at the bus stop though, gave me time to assess the evening and take in the situation that had just occurred. The bricks of guilt were still there, but now that the situation had come and gone, the feeling of betrayal began to set in. The whole ride home, I periodically glanced at my phone. To my amazement, Judi hadn't called me once. That gave me a sense of relief, because the last thing I needed was Conchita checking my phone and seeing Judi's number in the call log. I was in deep thought when suddenly the bus driver stopped the bus,

"This is your stop, right?" he asked.

"How'd you know?" I said with a puzzled expression on my face.

"I saw you on here with that pretty little black girl one day. Man, she's fine," he said boisterously. Considering what had just happened at the movies I became slightly agitated.

"Man, open the fuckin' door, and stop fuckin' watching me! Watch the fucking road!" I barked. Stunned, the bus driver just paused and stared at me with a bewildered look on his face.

"Damn young blood! I was just giving you a compliment, that's all," he said slowly opening the door.

Having felt bad for trippin' on the old man, I replied,

"My bad, I got a lot of shit on my mind. I didn't mean to go off on you like that. I'm sorry." After accepting my apology, he shook my hand, and I quickly darted off the bus.

Once inside of the house, I turned my attention to the fluorescent color microwave clock.

"11:30," I said to myself. The house was pitch-black, and I stumbled as I tried to navigate through the darkness. As I walked towards the bedroom, I began to get an uneasy feeling, so I paused and decided to detour into the bathroom instead. When I exited the shower, I felt cleaner than I did earlier, as if some of the guilt had been washed away. Then, while brushing my teeth, I heard Conchita calling me.

"Papi is that you?" she asked.

"Yeah baby, it's me," I replied somberly through the door. As I continued brushing, Conchita slipped into the bathroom behind me and wrapped her arms around my waist, sending a surge of warm energy through my entire body.

"I missed you Papi," she said as she kissed my back. Feeling immense guilt, I paused, looked in the mirror at her reflection, and leaned closer into her bosom.

"I missed you too, baby," I said still staring at her chocolate reflection.

Then I turned around, stared into her pain ridden face, and kissed her softly on the lips. When I pulled back, her eyes were still shut. Then she opened them slowly and said,

"Wow, Papi that was beautiful. What was that for?"

"You looked like you needed something to make you feel better," I told her.

"I did. Thanks," she softly said. I kissed her once more, then turned off the lights and followed her into the bedroom.

Black Devil-Blue Eyes

Chapter Ten
Secret Lies

"So, how we gonna' do this?" A raspy voice shouted from the dimly lit kitchen. Conchita trembled as the large dark man returned to the living room. His name was Chacho. His stature was gigantic, and his face was menacing like a snake waiting to pounce on a field mouse. The hideous scar across his left eye also made him terrifying to look at. The man shuffled around the small area like a lion circling its prey in the jungle.

"Bitch, I asked a muthafucking question!" he snarled. "I called you here to figure something out," he added staring at her intensely. Conchita was so terrified that she struggled to respond.

"I, I don't know what you want from me," she shot back. When she said that, his pacing temporarily stopped.

"Okay, so the reason I told your cousins to bring you here is because your brother owed me some money," he told her. Before he could finish his sentence, Conchita interrupted him.

"I can't get you any money. I'm a college student," she said trying to plead with him.

"Yes, this is true. You know, your brother used to talk about you being in college all the time," he retorted. "So, what you gonna do for me is work it off. You don't work right now do you?" He asked rhetorically. "Yes, you don't work, so I'm gonna give you the details, and you are gonna work for me until his debt is paid in full," he continued smiling grimly. "Every week, you gonna take a package to a different location," he said handing her a scrap piece of paper with an address on it.

"You want me to sell drugs?" Conchita said with a puzzled look on her face. The man turned and stared at her coldly before replying,

"No bitch, I don't want you to sell drugs. I want you to do my pick-ups. The money has already been arranged, all you got to do is go there, and they will give you the money. Get one of your cousins to roll with you; but chica, if the money doesn't reach me or if you try to grow a brain on me by calling the policia, just know that I know where your Madre' lives. Oh, and I heard your brother's in the ICU at Saint Paul's hospital. So, Mira' don't fuck around," he said sharply. Conchita looked at him with contempt, but she stuffed the scrap paper into her handbag, got up and headed for the door. As she hurried to exit the unit, Chacho stopped her and whispered in her ear,

"Mira, if it weren't for the amount of money that your brother owes me you wouldn't even be here," he said staring her down. Enraged, Conchita ripped away from his clutch and bolted out of the door. As she ran through the shit smelling hallway she began to sob profusely. When he seen her crying, Roberto got out of the car to comfort her.

"Mira, it's gonna be all alright," he said hugging her tightly. Feeling enraged by the sight of Conchita crying, Roberto stared sharply at the entrance of Chacho's building. After she was done crying she looked up at Roberto,

"Why the fuck don't you guys just kill him? She coldly asked. Shocked at the question, Roberto looked at her puzzled.

"We would, but Chi-Chi, he's got a lot of guys on the street. We don't have that kind of man power. We kill him and they kill you, your brother, auntie, me, and Manny.

They'd probably even kill that boyfriend of yours," he explained. Stunned by the repercussions that Roberto had just outlined for her, she stared at him helplessly.

"It's not fair," she whined as she continued to sob uncontrollably.

"I know Chi-Chi, I know," Roberto said as he held her tighter. "C'mon, be strong. I'm gonna drop you off back home, but Mira, don't tell that boyfriend of yours anything. You don't need him trying' to fix the problem. He'll only make things worse," he told her. She slowly shifted away from his hold, wiped her tear-stained face, and replied,

"Okay Berto I won't. I'm just gonna get this shit done and over with; but I'll tell you this, when I'm through and the debt is paid I'm gonna handle his ass." As Roberto slowly got into the car he paused briefly before asking her what she meant. She looked at him with a blank expression on her face but didn't say anything as she flopped onto the passenger seat.

"Mira, you better not do anything stupid. That guy isn't small time; he is dangerous," he said warning her. As Roberto continued to chastise her, suddenly Conchita snapped back.

"Look, Berto, I know you care for me, and you are trying to look out for me, but I'm a grown-ass woman. So, shut the fuck up!" Not wanting to further upset her, Roberto respected her wishes and didn't say anything. He just shot her a quick stare before shifting his focus back to the road.

When I awoke, I was shocked to find that Conchita wasn't lying next to me. It wasn't like her just to leave and not tell me where she was going. In my heart, I knew something was up. I looked at the clock, and it was 10:30 am. Maybe she went for breakfast, I reasoned in my head. Not wanting to brood over where she could've gone, I dismissed the thought and headed for the bathroom to freshen up. As I strolled down the hallway, I could hear the front door knob jiggle, then turn. It was Conchita. Before I could inquire about her whereabouts, she began to unload answers to the wondering questions in my head.

"Hey baby, I see your up. I went to check on my brother to see if his condition had gotten better. You looked so peaceful resting; I didn't want to disturb you. I know you'd be hungry when I got back, so I got you some breakfast from Waffle Palace. I even got the peanut butter bread you like so much," she said. At that moment, if I had any more inquiries, they were all dashed at the sight of the peanut butter bread.

"Damn baby, heat that up in the microwave. I'm gonna jump in the shower really quick, but I wanna fuck that up as soon as I get out," I told her. Then I raced to the room to grab my towel and bolted to the bathroom. As the beads of water ran off me, I could feel that something wasn't quite right.

After washing up, I slowly turned off the water and went through my daily grooming routine. When I finished in the bathroom, I swiftly moved to the bedroom to get dressed. Once I was satisfied with my attire I returned to the kitchen to devour the peanut butter bread. I threw the plastic container into the microwave, set the timer, and then turned to Conchita.

"Are you alright? I asked surveying her closely.

"Yeah, I'm cool. Why do you ask?" She replied.

"Just asking is all. You seemed different. I can feel something. It's like something's bothering you," I said. She shuffled the plastic fork into the container of eggs she was eating then stared at me,

"My brother being in the hospital is bothering me, and I'm really worried about him," she said. Feeling overwhelmed at the sight of her crying I quickly moved in close to comfort her.

"Oh, baby I'm so glad I have you. You are very sweet, I love you so much," she said trying to control her tears. I kissed her on the forehead and looked into her eyes.

"You know I'm here for you. Whatever you need, I got you. Since you don't have class today, why don't you try to relax? Everything's gonna be okay," I told her. Then I continued, "I'm late for my 9 o'clock class, but as soon as my last class ends I'll be back, okay?" She looked into my eyes and like a little child replied,

"Okay Papi." Feeling content, I kissed her lips once more and then left out to catch the bus.

While sitting in class, I couldn't help but think about Conchita. Something was wrong, but I couldn't put my finger on it. It seemed like she was holding something back that was far more pressing than just her brother laid up in the ICU, but if she didn't want to tell me then I wasn't going to stress it. As I tried to focus on the lecture, the thought of Conchita's saddened face kept gnawing at me. Not able to take it any longer, I abruptly got up and headed for the door.

"Mr. Sphinx, are you going somewhere?" the professor asked. "I'm not done yet explaining this theory," he continued.

"I'm sorry Mr. Ferrer, but I have an emergency," I said trying not to bring attention to myself.

"Well, if it's an emergency, then you have to tend to it I suppose," he said dismissing me. Feeling like the spotlight had just been placed on me; I quickly darted for the door. Once I was in the hallway, I quickly pulled out my cell and called Conchita. I expected to hear her voice after the first ring, but instead, it rang several times, and then went to her voicemail. After the beep, I left a message and then placed the phone back into my jacket pocket. While walking through the halls, I began to wonder what was going on with Conchita. I must have been in a daze, because I walked right past Judi, and didn't hear her yelling my name until she ran in front of me.

"Hey you, are you deaf or something?" She asked with a wide grin on her face.

"Oh, hey Judi, I didn't hear you. I gotta lot of shit on my mind is all," I said blankly.

"I yelled your name like five times. Is everything alright?" She asked.

"Yeah, I'm cool. Personal issues got me kinda bugged out," I replied.

"Well, you know I can make you feel a whole lot better," she said seductively.

"Look, Judi, I really gotta go," I said shoving past her. As I walked towards the exit, Judi just stood in the middle of the hallway watching me leave.

The bus ride seemed to take forever before it finally got to my stop. When it came to a complete halt, the doors took even longer to open. When they finally did, I immediately hopped off the bus and sprinted to the apartment. Once inside, I yelled for Conchita, but there was no reply. My heart began to grow with concern, and pound harder and harder as I scanned the entire unit looking for her. Growing more and more panicked; I rapidly took out my cell phone and called her. It rang and rang but there was no answer. *"Maybe I was tripping,"* I thought. *"Her brother was in intensive care, and her mother was in need of consoling,"* I continued to reason. *"But why is she not answering her phone though"*? I asked myself as if expecting to hear a reply. Feeling a sense of abandonment come over me, I hastily flopped onto the living room sofa. While I sat with my head in my lap, the silence in the room began to grow louder and louder. Then, all of a sudden, my phone rang.

"Yo, where are you?" I said, expecting to hear Conchita's voice on the other end.

"I'm at school, duh," said the voice on the other end. It was Judi.

"What do you want now Judi?" I asked.

"Damn! Look, I just wanted to know if you were going to be free next Wednesday to study. I wanna be ready for the next exam. There is no need to get all wound up," she fired back.

"Uh look, I'm going through some stuff right now, but I will let you know something by Sunday, okay?" I said rushing her off the phone. As she began talking, I didn't even bother to listen before hanging up on her. For the first time in a long time, I was alone, and it was eating at me. My heart was beating like a Congo drum, and I could feel my entire body pulsating. *"Maybe I was overreacting,"* I thought. Then I took a deep breath and made my way to the kitchen to pour myself a drink. I must've drunk damn near the whole bottle before drifting into a coma-like sleep.

When I came two, my cell phone was ringing off the hook.

"Hello," I drunkenly slurred.

"Hey Papi," said Conchita. "I know you're mad at me. I've been at the hospital all day with my mother. She's on pins and needles. I see you called, but right when I was about to call you back, my cell phone died," she explained. Having felt a great sense of relief, I replied,

"It's cool. I understand you're going through a lot, but baby you gotta communicate better. I hope your brother gets better, but babe what else is bothering you?" Then there was a brief pause before she replied,

"It's nothing. Why do you ask?" she said.

"You just seemed like you had more on your mind when you came in this morning. I've been around you long enough to tell when something is really fuckin' with you," I replied. Then there was another pause.

"No babe, there isn't anything else…For real," she said. The way she responded didn't sit well with me, but once again, if she wasn't going to tell me, then I wasn't gonna pry.

"Okay baby. Well when *are* you coming home?" I softly asked.

"I'll be home by noon Papi. Get some sleep, and try not to drink too much," she said as if she could smell the alcohol through the phone.

"I won't Mami, I won't," I said right before I blew a kiss through the phone and hung up. I wasn't satisfied with her answer to my lingering question, but what other choice did I have? I guess what she told me was going to have to suffice. Having heard Conchita's voice before the night was over, I peacefully stretched out across the couch and dozed back off.

Chapter Eleven
The devils are in the details

"Hey, you're even better than your brother," Chacho said while lighting up a cigarette. Then he looked her up and down coldly before continuing, "Your brother used to stop and get shit to eat, or fuckin' stop at a whore house. Muthafucker used to even dip into my money to have fun, but not you chica. You pick up, and you drop off. I like that. Now only seventy-six thousand more and you're home free," he said as he let out a sinister laugh. Conchita's face curled up at him in disgust.

"Yeah, whatever motherfucker," she coldly replied. Chacho didn't seem to mind her comment much, he just laughed at her as he counted the money.

"Look I know you're pissed. If it were my brother I'd be mad at a motherfucker like me too," he said while laughing at her. Then he continued, "But seriously chica, this is only business. This wasn't the first time your brother did this shit, but I can't keep letting things slide. This is how I fucking eat, and if a motherfucker keeps playing, then I gotta show 'em. Show 'em that I mean business." As she rose up from the cracked leather couch, Chacho leaned in near her.

"Here, take this," he said as he handed her a crumpled-up piece of paper. "Be there at eleven. Same drill, same shit. Get the money and come back to me." She grabbed the piece of paper out of his hand and looked at him with animosity.

"Yeah, yeah, I know, you dirty fuck," she said brushing past him to exit the apartment. As she neared the door, Chacho yelled at her,

"Just get my money bitch, and don't fuck up. Do you hear me bitch?"

Showing him no sign of acknowledgment, she flipped him the middle finger and kept walking. Once she got outside, she darted for Roberto's car.

"What did he say?" He scruffily asked.

"Nothing really, just the same shit. Hey, after a couple more pick-ups, why don't we just keep the money, get some guns and shut him down?" She asked seriously. Before answering, Roberto just looked at her. He took a deep breath before taking a cigarette out and lighting it up.

"Are you fuckin' crazy? That muthafucka will kill us. What part of that are you not getting?" He barked. Unsatisfied with his response she rolled her eyes.

"Man fuck all that. If we kill him, nobody's gonna want beef. They'll know we mean business...period. Look, I'm gonna do it whether you ride along with me or not. My mind is made up," she snapped. Having been given an indirect ultimatum, Roberto just took a deep pull from his cigarette,

"I'll ride with you, just gimme' the word, alright?" he told her. Then they looked at each other in agreement as the car cruised down the highway.

When I woke up, I expected to find Conchita nestled beside me. Instead what I found was a cold, empty spot in the bed where her body should've been. Pissed off; I looked at the alarm clock but realized it was only 9:30 am. I sighed in relief. She did say noon, I reasoned. I tried to lie back down, but couldn't fall back asleep, so I got up and headed to the bathroom. As I surveyed the cold in my eyes, I splashed hot water on my face. Today was a late day. I didn't have to be in class until one, so I took my time meticulously grooming myself. As I was getting into a rhythm brushing my teeth, I paused for a second thinking that I had just heard the front door open. So I placed my toothbrush down on the counter and rushed out of the bathroom to go investigate. Upon reaching the kitchen, I found Conchita standing near the kitchen sink opening a plastic container from Waffle Palace.

"Damn baby, you gotta' start announcing yourself. You startled the shit outta me," I said.

"Lo siento, baby," she said as she spun around and kissed me with her syrup-stained lips.

"You get me some?" I asked turning my attention to her food.

"Yeah, Papi I did. It's right here," she said motioning to another plastic bag on the counter.

"Damn baby, you're the best. But look, I'm gonna go freshen up. Why don't you join me," I said squeezing her ass.

"Okay Papi," she replied as she began undressing in the middle of the kitchen.

After making love in the shower, we returned to the kitchen to finish our food. As I placed my container in the microwave, I noticed something was missing.

"Hey, where's your little puppy?" I asked.

"You're just now noticing that the dog's gone?" she asked.

"Kind of," I stupidly replied.

"I gave it to my mother. She was feeling really down and out, so I gave it to her to comfort her," she said. "I didn't need it. I mean, I did like it, but he wasn't doing me any good. You should've seen my mother's face when I gave him to her. Her face lit up," she said with a half-broken smile. "I could tell that she really needed that dog," she continued. Trying to change the topic, Conchita then blurted out,

"Hey, when I leave the hospital, why don't we go see a movie later on this evening?" I missed seeing her, and I wanted to take her mind off her problems, so I happily obliged.

After we scarfed down our food, Conchita quickly grabbed her coat and darted for the door. Not wanting to see her go, I followed her out to the parking lot and planted one more kiss on her juicy lips. As I watched her get into her cousin's car, I suddenly felt a large lump rise in my throat. I felt choked up because I was beginning to see her less and less. These infrequent visits were starting to aggravate me. Having nothing else to do, I quickly headed back to the apartment.

Once inside, I plopped down on the sofa to watch some television. As soon as I turned on the T.V. my cell phone rang. It was Judi. I wasn't in the mood to talk, but I knew if I didn't answer my phone she'd just keep calling until I picked up. So, I answered.

"Hey, whatcha doing?" She asked.

"Shit, what's good?" I flatly said.

"Oh, nothing, I just wanted to see if you were free tonight. I'm having problems with my thesis paper, and I thought maybe you could help me out a little," she rambled on.

"Naw, not today, I got a lot of stuff going on. Maybe tomorrow, that'll probably be best," I said not really wanting to be bothered with Judi. Then there was a brief pause over the phone before she replied,

"Oh, okay, no problem. It's not like the paper is due next week. Well, call me when you get a chance," she said.

"Yeah alright," I coldly replied before hanging up the phone. Then I stared into space for a few minutes before turning my attention back to the television, *"something is wrong with Conchita,"* I thought. After what seemed like a few hours of mindless programming, I began to slip into a dazed and then eventually a deep nap.

When I awaken, it was 8 p.m. and I had missed my one o'clock class. Dismissing that fact, I grabbed my phone to see if Conchita had called me, but was shocked to find that I had no missed calls. Feeling slightly bothered, I called her phone. The line rang and rang with no answer before going to voicemail. Becoming puzzled, I hung up the phone without leaving a message. I sat in the living room feeling perplexed, because it was *her* idea to go see a movie, and now she was unreachable. Maybe I was tripping. Not wanting my mind to wonder, I lit up a cigarette and sat back on the couch trying to mellow out. As the silence and my thoughts began to grow louder, suddenly my phone rang.

"Hello," I answered trying to sound relaxed.

"I know you were in a bad mood earlier, so I was wondering if I could make you feel good," said Judi. Not having anything else to do I gave in.

"Fuck it, yeah okay," I said. I could tell that my response had made her night because she sounded as if she was gonna burst with excitement.

"Okay, well, I got my friend Brenda's car. I can pick you up in about twenty minutes, is that cool?" She asked.

"Yeah, that's cool," I said casually. After we made plans, I hung up the phone and continued staring into space. After a moment of silence, I picked up my phone and dialed Conchita's number one more time, but still no answer. Growing agitated; I tossed the phone onto the coffee table and stretched back out across the couch. I began flipping through the channels figuring it would be a while until Judi showed up, when suddenly there was a knock at the door.

"What the fuck?" I yelled having slightly been startled. When I got to the door and opened it, there was Judi, standing in the doorway. Wearing all pink, with a huge grin on her face.

"You ready to go?" she innocently asked. Surprised by the sight of her attire my mood shifted drastically.

"Yeah, let's bounce. Why the fuck you knock so damn hard, like you the fucking police!" I said as I fumbled for my keys trying to lock the door.

"I didn't mean to scare you," she said sarcastically.

"You didn't scare me. I just wasn't expecting you to bang on my door so hard," I said trying to downplay it.

"Next time I'll knock softer," she said as she leaned into me pressing her soft pink lips into mine.

"Come on, let's get to the car," I ordered. I didn't want to be seen with Judi if Conchita *did* pull up. When we reached the car, she tossed me the keys.

"You drive. I'm tired of driving. I've been driving around all day taking care of errands," she said. As I walked around to the driver side, Judi grabbed my pants and seductively said,

"Told you I wanted to make you feel good." I didn't need to ask as I could already tell what was on her mind. We both hopped inside, and as I started the ignition, her head dove into my lap. I quickly backed out, exiting the apartments and sped off.

As Conchita lay across her mother's lap, the doctor walked into the room. Not wanting to wake them, he hesitantly tapped her mother on the shoulder,

"Umm, Ms. Roseen," he said clearing his throat, "I have some bad news," he continued. Both Conchita and her mother's eyes begin to water as they anticipated hearing the worst.

"We're doing everything we can Ms. Roseen, but your son doesn't look like he'll pull through. He is stable for now, but he's in a vegetative state. We're just going to have to wait and see if he wakes up," he sternly said. After the doctor's prognosis of Ralph, Conchita and her mother began to cry uncontrollably. Having been through this drill before, it was obvious that the doctor still was unaccustomed to being the bearer of bad news. He just shuffled his papers, touched them both on the shoulder, and awkwardly walked off. Quickly realizing the doctor's insincerity, Conchita wiped the tears from her face.

"We will get through this Madre," she said.

After consoling her for several hours, Conchita was relieved when her mother finally drifted off to sleep. She then took out her cell phone and dialed Roberto. It rang a couple times before he scruffily answered,

"Mira it's 2:00 in the morning, what's up?" he asked.

"Yo, pick me up," she replied before hanging up the phone. She stroked her mother's face and pulled the hospital blanket over her shoulders before kissing her goodbye and exiting the room.

While she waited for Roberto outside, she took out a pack of kools, lit up a cigarette, and inhaled deeply. As soon as she took her last drag, Roberto pulled up.

Eager to escape the cold, she extinguished the half-smoked cigarette and opened the car door. Plopping down onto the crisp leather seats, she turned to Roberto,

"Can you get some guns?" she asked. Before answering her, he took a deep breath,

"Yeah I can get you some guns. What's the plan chica?" he asked as he bolted from the hospital lot.

As they flew down the expressway, Conchita lit up another cigarette.

"Well, the plan is for you to get the guns. I'm crashing at the hotel with you guys, and when that piece of shit Chacho calls me, we're gonna go over there. I'm gonna put a pistol in my purse since they always search my body. They never check my purse though. Five minutes after I get in there I'm gonna text you. I need y'all to hold a gun on the doorman so that when I drop Chacho, the doorman doesn't come in and blow my fucking head off. Then, before we go, you smoke the motherfucker at the door. You got that?" She sharply asked.

"Damn, how long have you been thinking about this?" Roberto asked with a grin on his face.

"A while now but fuck all that shit! Do you got the plan?" She snapped back.

"Yeah I got the plan Mira', chill!" Roberto calmly replied. As they continued down the highway, Conchita took out her phone and realized that she had two miss calls from George. She quickly cleared her phone log. She missed being with him, but she didn't need any distractions with what she was about to attempt. As she zoned out, Roberto continued rambling. Not paying him any mind, she looked out the window over the city scenery.

"Home of the brave," she thought. That's just what she was going to have to be to pull this off.

After the movie, Judi dropped me off at my apartment. It must've been around 1:30 in the morning when we pulled up to my unit because it was 10:30 p.m. when we caught our movie.

"Thanks for the company. I've wanted to see that movie for the longest, but I didn't want to see it by myself," she softly said before I exited the car.

"Oh, no problem. It ain't like I was busy or anything. It was a good movie," I replied. I was lying. Between getting head in the car, and head in the theater, I didn't remember any of the it. Then while walking towards my apartment Judi yelled,

"Can I get that dick anytime?" she asked.

"Maybe," I said as I continued heading towards my apartment. Upon opening the door, I noticed that the house was dead silent. I took my jacket off and examined my phone, but there still weren't any calls from Conchita. Feeling puzzled, I tossed my coat on the couch and headed towards the bedroom to get some much-needed sleep. As I lay on the bed waiting to drift off to sleep, I couldn't shake the feeling that a void was beginning to set in. Not seeing Conchita regularly was causing me to become more and more distant. I was hoping that Conchita wasn't pondering the same thing. If she was, where would we go from here? Was this the beginning of the end? Not wanting to dwell on the idea anymore, I closed my eyes and fell asleep.

Black Devil-Blue Eyes

Chapter Twelve
The devil's wrath

Roberto had managed to get a whole arsenal within ten hours. He and Conchita hardly went to sleep the night before. Roberto spent most of the night calling around for favors, and getting illegal guns in New York was no easy feat. By the time Conchita hopped in the shower and returned to the living room, Roberto had every gun spread out across the coffee table.

"Damn Berto, we only need a few guns, not a whole damn gun store," Conchita barked. Not having much of a reply, Roberto just stood there dumbfounded scratching his head.

"With who you're going up against you're lucky if you don't need a whole fleet of guns," he replied. Then there was a brief pause while Conchita surveyed the table,

"Okay, if you say we need 'em, I'm gonna take your word for it," she said. Then she continued, "So here's the plan. It's Thursday. I always get a delivery Thursday, so when he calls me, we head over there. He always gives me the address on a crumbled paper because he doesn't like talking over the phone. When we get there, you and Manny stand outside and wait five minutes after I go in. I was going to text you but that might cause alarm. So, wait five minutes. After I blow his head off, shoot the doorman. You got it?"

There was a brief pause as Roberto and Manny just looked at each other before answering her. After the quick plan, Conchita pulled out three black ski masks from her purse.

"Here," she said tossing Manny and Roberto a mask.

"Damn Chica, you're not playing around. Where'd you get these?" Roberto asked curiously.

"The surplus shop," Conchita replied. Then she continued, "Look, I'm tired as fuck. Manny go check on mama, I'm gonna crash here on the couch till Chacho calls me. That should be about ten. Don't wake me up until nine." Manny did as he was told and hurried out of the apartment while Roberto retreated to his room. Feeling exhausted, Conchita plugged up her phone charger, set the alarm clock on her cell phone, and curled up on the couch.

9 o'clock seemed to have come as soon as Conchita closed her eyes. Her cell phone alarm clock was blaring so loud that it caused Roberto to wake up and rip the blanket off her,

"Hey Chi-Chi, wake up. It's nine o'clock; time to get ready!" He shouted. Feeling dazed and half asleep, Conchita slowly sat up. After lighting a cigarette, she went into the bathroom to change clothes. When she returned to the living room, Roberto tossed her a .38 revolver.

"Check the chamber, chica. Make sure it's loaded," he casually said. Without a word, Conchita did as she was told. After checking their weapons, everyone sat back and waited for the call. When 10 o'clock rolled around, almost like clockwork, her cell phone began to ring loudly.

"Yeah, what's up," Conchita calmly said.

"You need to come see me tonight, don't you chica?" Chacho snarled.

"Be there in twenty minutes," she replied. Then she hung up the phone, looked at Roberto and Manny and asked, "You guys ready?" Both men just nodded as they grabbed their coats from the rack.

Before leaving the apartment, they tucked their guns into their waistbands then headed for the door.

When they arrived outside of Chacho's building, Conchita's hands were shaking uncontrollably. Roberto noticed this, and before she could open the car door he grabbed her arm,

"Mira, we don't have to do this if you're not ready," he told her. Trying to regain her nerves she took a deep breath.

"No, I'm cool. He's gonna pay," she replied. Then she flung open the door and hopped out of the car. As she strolled through the breezeway, she noticed that no one was standing outside of the door. Her heart sank, and she stopped walking. Trying to regain her courage, she took another breath, zipped her jacket up, and continued walking towards the apartment. When she knocked on the door, she could hear Chacho screaming at the top of his lungs. He must've been cussing someone out over the phone. Trying not to get cold feet, she stood stationary taking in deep breaths as the drafty wind blew through the breezeway. As she waited for him to answer the door, she began growing increasingly nervous; almost to the point of turning away and scrapping her plan. Soon as she turned to walk away, Chacho answered the door. Before letting her in, he suspiciously looked her up and down, then peered down the breezeway and quickly snatched her inside.

"Damn, your paranoid fuck! Chill the fuck out!" She sharply quipped. Chacho didn't pay her any attention. He just went through the routine of handing her a crumpled piece of paper while lighting up a cigarette. Trying to appear normal, Conchita took the scrap piece of paper and stuffed it into her purse. Then there was an awkward moment between the two, as Chacho expected her to dart out of the apartment as she always did, but she didn't.

"What the fuck you waiting for bitch?" Chacho growled. "Don't you have something to do?" He continued.

"Yeah motherfucker, I do," Conchita shouted back. Then she pulled out the revolver and fired two rounds point blank into Chacho's chest. He must've been an animal though, because as soon as he was hit, he lunged at her as his blood was spraying everywhere. However, his body couldn't sustain the two shots, and he quickly collapsed onto the floor. As he lay there bleeding, he clutched his chest groaning in agony trying to fight the inevitable.

Right on cue, Roberto burst into the apartment but stood for a minute in shock. He looked at Chacho's lifeless body, then refocused his attention back on Conchita.

"Mira, we gotta go. Move your ass!" Still in disbelief, she just stood there watching Chacho taking his last breath. Realizing the cops would be coming soon, she quickly lowered her gun and ran out of the apartment. As they bolted to the car, none of them wore their mask. This would prove to be their undoing.

Once she was inside the car she stuffed the revolver into her purse, quickly took out a cigarette, and lit it up. Roberto started the engine, and without even turning on the heat shifted into drive and sped off into the night. As fast as Roberto was driving, it seemed as if it took only a matter of minutes to get back to the hotel.

Once they were inside the scattered room, they all plopped on the couch.

"Shit Conchita, you really did that shit. I thought you were just talking, but you really did that shit!" Roberto said.

Still in shock from what she had just done, Conchita just stared at Roberto with a blank look on her face. Manny went into the kitchen to retrieve some glasses and a bottle of Tequila.

"Roberto, chill the fuck out, please. Look, what we're gonna do is have a drink and relax," said Manny when he returned to the living room.

"You right, you right," Roberto said as he sat down holding his cup. While Manny began filling everyone's glass, Conchita set hers' aside to rifle through her purse in search for her phone. Upon finding it, she quickly called George. Instead of hearing his voice, the phone just rang and rang, before finally going to voicemail. Disappointed that he hadn't answered, she sighed and left a message. After hanging up, she just stared into space holding her glass. She mechanically took sips of her tequila, as the magnitude of what she had just done came crashing down like a ton of bricks. Then the thought of George not answering his phone began to gnaw at her. Had I been that distant to him? she thought. Tomorrow I'm going to see my baby. Put everything on hold and spend some quality time, she continued. Not wanting to dwell on her racing thoughts any longer, she took another swig of her drink and stretched out across the couch.

As soon as she closed her eyes, it was the next day. The sun beamed through the blinds causing her to wake up almost immediately. She checked her call list, but still no calls from George.

"Fuck!" She snapped. "Hey, Berto let me borrow your car," she shouted.

"Whatever! Just leave me alone," Roberto yelled back, still hungover from the night before. Conchita jumped up, threw on her shoes, snatched his keys off the coffee table, and bolted for the door.

Wanting to catch George before he left for his first class, she drove like a bat out of hell.

When she pulled into the apartment complex, she checked her watch for the time. 8:10. George didn't leave for his 10 o'clock class until 9:20, she thought. Once she opened the front door, she could hear the shower running in the bathroom. Wanting to surprise him, she quietly slipped inside, discarded her clothes, and headed for the shower. When she pulled back the shower curtain, George turned around surprise,

"Conchita," he said. As the bathroom filled with steam, she stepped inside joining him under the faucet while the water drenched her naked body. As she held him close, she closed her eyes and imagined the water washing away her deeds from last night.

After showering, we headed for the bedroom to get dressed.

"I tried calling you the day before, but you didn't pick up. What's going on Chi-Chi? Is something the matter?" I asked.

"No, everything's fine. Just been spending time with my mother. She's in really bad shape, and my brother's in a coma, but other than that I'm okay," Conchita said while putting on her panties. For a few seconds, I just stood there dumbfounded. I began to feel shitty for not being more considerate. So, to clean up my mess, I started back paddling.

"My bad, it's just that I've called you several times and you didn't pick up. It feels like you've checked out of the relationship, or that you're keeping something from me," I told her. The last part of what I said must've struck a nerve because she stared at me with a look of horror on her face that I had never seen before. Growing worried I prodded further,

"Chi-Chi what is going on? Why did you just look at me like a deer in headlights just now?" I asked. Shuffling to put her shirt on, she turned her back to me.

"Nothing is wrong baby, okay?" she replied. Not feeling entirely satisfied, I walked around the bed and pulled her close to me. As I held her, she began to cry uncontrollably.

"It's gonna be okay Mami. Your brother's gonna pull through," I said stroking her hair

"Thank you, baby, you don't know how much I needed to hear that," she said looking up at me with her big puppy dog eyes.

Realizing it was nearing 9:20, I continued getting dressed and arranged to hook up with her after I got out of my last class. Then, I quickly kissed her lips and raced for the door.

After my last class had come and gone, I called Conchita to see where she was so that we could hook up. When she answered the phone, I could barely understand what she was saying as she was crying uncontrollably.

"Baby, what's wrong? What happened?" I frantically asked.

"My brother is dead Papi," she said continuing to cry hysterically.

"Baby, baby calm down, I'm on my way home. We're gonna get through this. Everything is gonna be all right," I said, reassuring her.

"Okay, Papi," she sobbingly replied.

When I got home, she was gone. I searched every room, even the patio, but nothing. She was nowhere in sight. Feeling a little befuddled, I quickly called her phone. When she answered, I began to sound off,

"Baby, where are you? I raced straight to the house, and then I get here, and you're gone. What the fuck?"

"I'm at my mother's house. She was having a meltdown, so I came here to comfort her, and to help make funeral arrangements. I'm so sorry I didn't tell you anything, but she called me back after I talked to you. Once I got here, I had to pull it together because she was *way* more distraught than I was. I meant to call you back, to tell you that I was over here, but dealing with her, I guess it just kinda slipped my mind. Los siento Papi," she said seeming un-phased by my questioning.

"It's okay baby, I feel you. You gotta be there for your mom. I totally understand," I replied. Even though I said it, I didn't mean it. This routine of rarely seeing Conchita was starting to become bothersome. However, trying to be considerate, I just swallowed my pride and made the best of the situation.

"Well, when *am* I going to see you?" I asked.

"Wednesday Papi, the funeral is Wednesday. Wear something black and meet me at Saint Marcus Cemetery on 15th and Christianson," she replied.

"Oh, okay. I'll see you there," I said flatly trying not to come off selfish. Then we said our goodbyes, and I hung up the phone.

Now, the void that seemed to move in slow had cruised right up and landed in the vacant spot of my heart. As I sat there, letting the rage consume me, suddenly my phone rang.

"What!" I yelled, without looking at the caller ID. After a brief pause I instantly knew who it was. It was Judi.

"Uhh, are you okay?" She sweetly asked.

Now usually when Judi called, I'd tend to be sour the whole time, but after a few weeks of sparsely seeing Conchita, I was now beginning to get used to her. I mean, she was still annoying, but it almost was like a convenience of sorts.

"My bad, what's good, Judi?" I flatly asked.

"Well, I need help writing this summation essay and I was wondering if you'd come over tomorrow and kinda help me out," she said. After what went down at the movies between her and I, I kind of felt like she was scheming. So, I went along with her.

"Yeah, I can help you. What time? I have classes till 6:45 tomorrow," I told her.

"8 o'clock works for me. Does that work for you?" she asked. Since most of my school project deadlines had been met, I figured why not? She *was* sexy, and I *was* starting to get bored at the house by myself, so I obliged.

"Yeah, that works for me. I'll hit you up after my last class and make my way over there," I said.

"Well, if you want, I can pick you up, so you don't have to ride the bus," she replied.

"Alright, cool," I said. After saying our goodbyes, I quickly hung up the phone and stretched out across the couch.

Black Devil-Blue Eyes

Chapter Thirteen
Devils are angels too

The next day had come almost as soon as I closed my eyes. It seemed as if it was fate that I was supposed to meet with Judi. While sitting in class, the hours seemed to just drop off the clock. Preoccupied with thoughts of Conchita, I was having a hard time concentrating during my class lectures. I just zoned out. The subconscious part of my brain was on auto-pilot, just scribbling notes robotically. At the end of my last class, I hadn't even left the room before Judi was blowing my phone up.

"Yo, what up?" I somberly asked.

"Aw, nothing. Just seeing where you were at. I'm in the parking lot," she blurted out.

"Damn I haven't even left my classroom yet. Yo, you hyper as fuck!" I coldly said.

"Is that a problem?" She rhetorically asked.

"Whatever, I'll be out there in a minute," I sharply replied.

When I got outside, Judi was sitting in the front seat fidgeting with her cell phone, but as I approached the car, she quickly looked up. Her face lit up like a Christmas tree full of lights. As I walked towards the car she popped the locks, and I got inside plopping down onto the seat.

"How were your classes?" she asked as soon as I sat down.

"Cool," I said flatly.

"Okay," she replied. Not wanting to talk, I just remained silent as the car sped away from the campus.

Upon entering her apartment, she quickly dashed to the kitchen.

"You wanna drink?" she blurted out. I had a lot on my mind, so I figured why not.

She poured us both a drink in the kitchen, and then spun around like a ballerina, when she returned to the living room.

"So, you know, I kind of lied about the paper. I don't need any help with it. I'm already finished with it," she said giggling. Then she continued, "I just like you, and I really wanted to see you. I don't know why I like you, but I do. I mean you're an asshole most of the time, but you can be chill when you want to be." My first reaction was to cuss her out, but being as I was growing lonely at my place; I swallowed my drink and continued to listen. I'm not gonna lie, it kinda felt good having someone around. Even if that other person just wanted to fuck. But instead of spilling out my guts, I just drank, and tried to have a good time.

We were talking and joking when all of a sudden, Judi abruptly got up and headed to her bedroom. When she returned, she was wearing a bright pink G-string and a small tank top. Having been alone mostly for the past several weeks, and not having much physical contact with Conchita, I grabbed Judi's hand and pulled her down on me. As I rubbed over every inch of her soft flesh, I began passionately kissing her body all over. Then, she pulled off my shirt, unbuckled my belt, and began stroking my dick.

"Let's go to my room," she said whispering in my ear. Obeying her request, I quickly lifted her off the couch and carried her into the bedroom.

The next day, feeling hungover, I was awakened by the smell of breakfast cooking in the kitchen. Feeling a ferocious hunger come over me, I scrambled to where the smell was emanating from.

When I entered the kitchen, Judi was standing stationary over the stove, wearing nothing but a smile.

"Hey, you're up," she said as she hurriedly stirred the eggs. After pouring them into the skillet, she quickly kissed me and returned her attention back to the eggs so as not to burn them. Feeling the room starting to spin, I retreated to the living room and patiently waited for my breakfast. As soon as I sat down, Judi was entering the living room with food in tow. When she lowered the plate, I began to dig in.

"Damn, this is a good ass breakfast! Either I'm hungry as hell, or this is the best breakfast I ever had," I said stuffing food into my face. While eating like a madman, and complementing Judi in between bites, she hardly said anything. She just sipped her tea and sat back watching me. After eating, I was too full to do anything. I just sat back and turned on the television, attempting to squeeze in a little cat nap. Judi must've wanted to get a little closer because she laid her head on my lap and closed her eyes.

After an hour or so, the heat from each other's bodies must've awakened us because we woke up rubbing on each other's private parts like wild animals. Then Judi started giving me head so good that I just sprawled out across the couch. She gave me, what seemed like an eternity of fellatio, that I hungrily reciprocated, straddling her hips around my face. When that became too steamy, we both dove onto the carpet for more spacious room. What seemed like an hour of thrusting may have only been twenty minutes, but once we finished our naked bodies just collapsed onto the floor. Then, it was time for nap number two.

When we finally woke up, this time to be more active, we both headed for the bathroom. Once the water was running we climbed into the shower and stood under the faucet letting the water fall onto, then bead off our bodies. We made out for a little while then exited the shower to lay on the bed naked.

"How come you're more open to coming over lately?" Judi asked.

"Because I haven't been busy," I said fishing for answers. Judi looked at me unconvinced.

"What about your girlfriend? How are you able to just hang out with me without her caring?" she shot back. Not wanting to divulge too much to Judi, I kept it short and sweet.

"She's been very preoccupied with family matters that don't concern me, is all," I told her. Then I grabbed a joint off her nightstand and continued,

"But yo, don't ask me about shit like that," I barked.

"Damn, my bad," Judi replied looking slightly perturbed.

After a few more hours of lounging, we then got up and begin to get dressed. Afterwards, I went into the living room to watch some television while Judi began cleaning the kitchen and other areas of her apartment. Becoming exhausted with lame programs, Judi threw on her shoes and offered to take me back to my apartment. I accepted her offer, and after grabbing our jackets, we headed to the car.

Judi floored it all the way until we got to my apartment parking lot. After putting the car in park, she then turned her attention to me,

"So, can we keep doing this?" she asked with a mischievous smile on her face. Kind of expecting the question, I didn't even hesitate to respond.

"Yeah, we can keep doing this, but only until shit gets back to normal for me. Then we'll have to chill out," I said. Appearing to be processing what I had just told her, she seductively stared at me for a brief second,

"Okay," she replied. Then she leaned over and kissed me before popping the car locks. Not wanting to be spotted by any of my nosey neighbors, I quickly hopped out of the car and headed for my apartment. As soon as I entered the house, my phone rang.

"Hello," I casually answered.

"Hey, Papi, what you doin'?" Conchita asked. Before I could answer, I felt a rush of guilt flood my entire body.

"Nothing much, just chillin' and going over some notes," I said.

Then there was a brief silence before she replied,

"Well I probably won't see you until the funeral. It'll be Wednesday. My mothers' a mess. This whole situation Papi, got me discombobulated but I'm trying to keep it together for her," she said.

"I understand Mami," I told her, but that was a lie. I didn't understand. Nobody in my family had ever died from a fatal accidental. I absolutely didn't care. All I knew is that I was growing increasingly lonely with not having anyone to spend time with. I shallowly tried to relate throughout the entire conversation, before ending it with an even shallower farewell. That was Sunday night.

Between classes, projects, and hanging out with Judi, I had lost track of the days. When I finally looked at my phone calendar, it was Thursday.

"Oh shit!" I shouted. I had forgotten all about the funeral. What was even stranger was the fact that Conchita hadn't even called to remind me, or to see why I never attended.

Monday:

While sitting in a dimly lit interrogation room, a loud voice snarled across from Conchita,

"Look, we know your brother was involved with Chacho, and now he's dead," the detective told her. We pulled Chacho's phone records, and you know what we kept seeing chica? Your number kept popping up. Now, why is that?" the detective asked.

"Okay, after my brother was hospitalized, I got a call from Chacho. He told me that he wanted me to pay back the money my brother owed. I don't have that kind of money I told him. He told me to meet him somewhere, and I did. From there he asked me for sexual favors in exchange for the money. He would call me, we'd hook up and fuck, and that's it. He said if I fucked him until he was satisfied, then my brother was in the clear," Conchita told him. Stunned by her false revelation, the detective continued to prod her,

"Well why didn't you come forth with this information earlier?" he asked.

"He said if I did, he would kill me, my Madre, and if my brother hadn't died yet, that he would have someone put poison in his IV," she replied nonchalantly. "Man, I just did what I was told because I didn't want anything more to happen to my family. As for him being dead, I don't know anything about that. Sorry for him," she continued.

Half-heartedly believing her story, the cop sat there for a few minutes before continuing to question her,

"Well, where were you the night he was murdered?" he asked.

"What night was that?" she said pretending to be puzzled.

"The 22nd of this month," the cop fired back without breaking stride.

"I would've been at my cousin's hotel," she said as if she were recollecting her whereabouts. She knew from watching forensic shows, that they had probably traced her phone's location. They did.

"Okay, I'm going to ask you to sit in the hall," he told her. After getting up from the table, he then motioned at the two-way mirror to bring Roberto in from the other room. As she sat in the hallway her mind began to wonder whether Manny or Roberto would crack under pressure. She knew they were stand-up guys, but she also knew that killing Chacho was *her* idea, and if anyone was to blame for this situation it was her.

After six grueling hours of interrogation, the door finally swung open and Manny strolled out like he didn't have a care in the world. Moments later, Roberto appeared from the room across the hallway. While interrogating Roberto, they had moved him to another room so that they could bring in Manny to cross up his story, but it didn't work. As all three begin putting on their coats, the detective issued a stern warning,

"This ain't over! I know one of you motherfuckers are involved with this in some way, shape, form or fashion. I just can't prove it now, but I will. If anyone of you gets found out, your gonna get the max! You hear me? The max!" he shouted.

"Yeah, whatever cop!" they all replied while shuffling towards the door. Then they ushered themselves out of the precinct lobby, and that was that. Or, so they thought.

Tuesday had come and gone, and I didn't hear a word from Conchita all day. Nor did I even try to call her. I know I was being selfish, but to go from having someone there to vaguely seeing them was starting to annoy me.

Wednesday night came, and since Conchita was consoling her mother and dealing with family affairs, I took the liberty of inviting Judi over. I forgot all about Conchita. That was a bad idea, because Thursday night, while Judi and I were up naked, smoking a joint, I heard the door unlock. My heart sunk into my stomach, and Judi stared at me in silence. Feeling totally shocked, I didn't even try to get up, as I was paralyzed with fear. I just sat there completely stunned.

When Conchita hit the bedroom doorway, she must've been as shocked as Judi and me, because she didn't even say anything. She just stood there staring at us in disbelief. Her shock quickly wore off though, because she quietly turned around and headed straight to the kitchen. I could tell she was searching for a knife because the sound of kitchenware began to clank loudly. As I got up to throw my pants on, Judi was halfway dressed and heading towards the door. She would've made it out of the room, except that Conchita was just a little quicker.

Upon reaching the doorway, Conchita blocked Judi's path and punched her square in the face, causing her to hit the floor. The punched instantly leveled Judi, and she was out for the count. Conchita then turned her attention to me, pulling a large knife from her waistband.

"Hey Mami, calm down," I said, but she wasn't trying to hear me out. She just kept inching towards me. I pleaded with her to talk it out, when suddenly she stopped and re-tucked the knife. Then standing in the middle of the room, she looked at me with a bewildered look on her face,

"I've been going through this shit about my brother, my distraught mother, and this is how you treat me? You know I wouldn't have been away from you so much if it wasn't important. You know that! You didn't even come to the fuckin' funeral! You said fuck me, then turned around and fucked this bitch in *our* place. But you know what? Get your shit and get the fuck out, before I cut your dick off motherfucker!" she screamed. Before I exited the room, I picked Judi up off the floor, grabbed a few things, then left the apartment.

Once we got outside I helped Judi get into the passenger seat, then I got inside the driver's seat and started the car. As I backed out of the parking lot, the magnitude of what had just happened began to sink in. I cruised down the street, and as I drove, finally came to grips that it was over. I was in shock the whole drive to Judi's place.

When I arrived, I quickly found a parking spot and slowly helped Judi out of the car. It looked like she was still dazed, from that hook to the face. Annoying as she could be at times, I felt bad for her. She hadn't done anything to deserve being punched like that. It was *my* fault entirely. Since Judi seemed to be half conscious, I scooped her up and carried her into the apartment.

When we entered inside, I didn't even look for a light switch. I just rushed to the couch, plopped her down, and retreated for our belongings in the car. It only took me a few minutes, but when I returned, Judi was completely asleep with dry blood plastered all over the side of her face. As she slept, I just stared at her lying there, *"Damn!"* I thought. I felt bad for her, and I felt embarrassed for myself. Trying to shake it off, I went to retrieve a blanket for Judi then headed to the kitchen to pour myself a much-needed drink. I had seriously fucked up. The funny thing about it though, as much as I loved Conchita, the distance between us over past several weeks made it easier to deal with. As I began to doze off, my phone beeped loudly from a text message. It was Conchita, and it read:

"I really fucking loved you! Come and get the rest of your shit tomorrow or else I'm going to burn it, motherfucker!" I didn't even have any fight in me to respond in depth.

"Okay. I'll be there at one o'clock. I love you too," I simply replied. Then I tossed my phone onto the floor, placed my glass on the table and curled up against Judi's soft hips.

Chapter 14
Resuming with broken pieces

When I woke up, Judi was hustling and bustling cooking away in the kitchen. As good as the food smelled, I was kind of shocked that she was cooking for me, considering she had just taken a right hook to the face *because* of me. So before asking her what she was cooking, I surveyed her eye and then proceeded with my questions.

"Are you okay?" I curiously asked. From her demeanor you would've assume that she had been through that before, and you would've been right.

"I'm good, are you?" she softly said. For a minute I was thrown for a loop, because that wasn't the response I was expecting. I expected her to be pissed off, yelling at me and telling me to leave but none of that happened. She just looked at me and smiled.

"I am okay. It ain't the first time a chick kicked my ass! And it won't be the last time," she said giggling while continuing to scramble eggs. Feeling kind of awkward about her response, I walked over to her, kissed her forehead, then grabbed a plate. When I sat down, Judi began shoveling eggs onto my plate while placing more items in front of me. I sat there chewing dumbfoundedly searching for something to say but nothing came to me, so, I just continued chewing in silence.

After attacking my big ass breakfast, I just sat there. I wasn't really bothered by what had just transpired between Conchita and I as much as I was confused, but I was perplexed at Judi's reaction.

"Yo, what is up with you? You ain't pissed at me, at all?" I said after about twenty minutes of starring in a daze.

"No, I'm good. How come you keep asking?" she said. Beginning to grow frustrated I snapped,

"If it was me, I'd be pissed off!" I growled. Then there was a brief pause before she replied,

"Well it's *not* you. I mean, I kind of knew that eventually something would go down, and we didn't make it any better chillin' in your spot like it was all good. That type of shit usually happens." "Plus, I *was* fucking you and you *were* in a relationship. Can't be mad at what I had coming," she continued. Her explanation of the whole situation was unbelievable but it was going to have to suffice. Then there was a brief silence between us before she took a deep gulp of her orange juice and casually asked,

"So, you wanna stay here for a while? I mean since your girl threw you out and all." Relieved by the fact that I didn't have to ask, I quickly accepted her offer. Now that it seemed that everything between us was okay, I got up from the table and set my plate into the sink.

"Around one, ima' take off to get my stuff," I calmly said before turning towards the bathroom. She nodded her head, kissed me on the cheek, and then headed into the living room to watch T.V. Then, I immediately darted to the bathroom to freshen up.

After taking a shower and putting on my clothes, I quickly headed for the door. As I raced outside, I noticed that Judi hadn't even bother to say goodbye. Not putting any stock into the idea, I just dismissed the it and darted for the bus stop.

Once I got to Conchita's place, I noticed there were a few patrol cars outside. When I approached the door, two line-backer sized officers were escorting Conchita out in handcuffs.

"What's going on?" I asked puzzled by the scene. The cops didn't even answer me. They just casually asked me to step aside and told me to go to the precinct to find out any further information.

"Tell my Madre," Conchita said as she was walking by. Stunned, I looked at her and the officers as they briskly shuffled towards a squad car. Once they pulled off, I headed inside and began filling up a suitcase.

After I was done, I called Conchita's mother like she had asked me to. As the phone rang, I began recalling the last several weeks and how Conchita was M.I.A. *"What had she done?"* I thought. Even worst, who had she done it with? When her mother picked up, I began shooting off everything I had just seen. I told her what precinct to go to, but when she asked me who to speak with, and how much the bail amount was, I drew a blank.

"They didn't tell me any of that Ma," I flatly said. Then there was a brief pause before she began crying uncontrollably. I tried to console her but to no avail, she just kept crying. Feeling like a piece of shit for what had transpired between me and Conchita the night before, I just hung up the phone.

The whole time I was on the bus I was in a daze. I couldn't believe Conchita was in jail. Just the thought of her in custody was blowing my mind. The bus ride seemed to take an eternity but when I got to Judi's place, my phone began ringing like crazy. I looked down, and at first didn't recognize the number, but when I answered, I realized it was Conchita calling from county lock up.

"Yo what up," I answered.

"Nothing's up," she snapped. "Look, I need to know why you were fucking that bitch. I mean it ain't like I was neglecting you on purpose and shit!" she continued.

"Cause, you were always fucking gone! I mean, everyday coming home from school, sitting at the house missing you. It's like you separated me from your family and I just got sick of that shit! The distance was setting in, and I just stop giving a fuck," I told her. "Anyways, what the fuck did you do?" I continued. There was a brief pause before she replied,

"I can't talk about that right now. My Madre' is going to post my bail and I'll be out Monday," she coldly told me. I didn't even have a response to what she had just said. I just sat there with the phone to my face feeling stupid. Then, as I was about to tell her that I still loved her, the phone cut off.

The next couple of weeks were weird and I was in limbo bouncing back from school to Judi's spot. I never got any information if Conchita was out, and when I went over to her apartment she was never there.

Then one day as I was walking down the street, coming from the local bar, I ran into her mother.

"Hey ma," I said. She looked for a second and squinted her eyes before recognizing me. When she finally did, tears begin to stream down her face and she smiled.

"Oh George, where have you been?" she asked. Before I could answer she began flooding me with news, "Chi-Chi was sentenced to 6 years in prison for accessory to murder of some drug dealer," she told me.

Shocked by the news, I just stood there in a daze. *"What the fuck had Conchita been up too? And what did she have to do with a drug dealer?"* I thought to myself. As I toiled the thought around in my head, it suddenly clicked. Her brother was hit by someone, and in the newspaper the police did say that they didn't believe it was an accident.

As she babbled on, I just stood there taking in the news about Conchita. Now I felt even worse about how things ended between her and I. Not only had her brother been killed, but I cheated on her and now she was locked up. Damn, I really hadn't been a good boyfriend. I felt like a piece of shit.

After a few minutes of zoning out, I snapped back and began to focus on what Conchita's mother was saying.

"Hey ma I got to go, but you take care of yourself, and if you talk to Conchita, tell her I love her," I said.

"You can tell her yourself. She's at the county lock up over on 177th St. She'll be there two more days until they ship her upstate," she shouted as I darted across the street.

"Okay, I'ma do that. Thanks ma!" I replied. As soon as I hit the curb my bus was pulling up. When the doors opened, I fumbled for my bus pass and hopped on. As I sat there thinking, the bus began picking up speed and quickly darted down the road.

When I got back to Judi's house I entertained the thought of going to visit Conchita when all of a sudden Judi walked through the door.

"What's up?" she curiously asked. Not really wanting to talk about what was on my mind, I quickly switched topics.

"Hey, are you cooking tonight?" I asked. Realizing what I had just done she paused and stared at me before answering.

"Oh, I see. I don't know, I was thinking about it. Why? What you want to eat for dinner tonight?" she casually said.

"I don't care as long as it's good," I flatly replied. Then there was a brief silence in the living room before she took out some weed and rolling papers.

"You know if you're still fucked up over your ex I understand. You look like you've been thinking about her every day," she said.

"I'm fine. It ain't her that's been on my mind it's all these classes," I told her. I was lying, and Judi could tell but she didn't press the issue. She just looked at me slyly as she licked her joint.

Later on, after the big meal Judi had cooked, I laid on the couch stuffed. As I zoned out watching T.V., Judi entered the room frolicking around in a white negligee'. Catching my attention, I instantly sat up and pulled her onto the couch. As we began to feverishly rub each other down, I pinned Judi underneath me and proceeded to take out my pinned-up frustrations on her. Being that she didn't mind it rough, I didn't even try to slow down. I just went hard for a good while. After what seemed like an eternity and an eruptive climax, I flopped back onto the couch and dozed off into a coma like sleep.

Days passed and it wasn't until a week had gone by, that I realized I had missed the chance to see Conchita before she was shipped upstate. Since there wasn't anything else I could do, I just hung my head low and continued walking to the bus stop. It seemed like a long bus ride home, but once I got to the apartment I quickly entered inside and took refuge into the living room. As I laid across the couch, I began thinking about Conchita. Wondering how she was holding up and how she had gotten herself involved with murder.

Chapter 15

When heaven collapses

It seemed as if the months had fallen off the calendar by the time my graduation came around. When the day arrived, everyone was there. From my family to part of Conchita's family. Which I thought was kind of odd, considering how she and I ended. After the ceremony, Conchita's mother rushed up to me and gave me a hug.

"You will always be Familia no matter what," she whispered in my ear before letting me go. Then she kissed me on the cheek, wobbled through the crowd and out of the auditorium. I hadn't really thought about Conchita that much, but it was at that moment that my mind flashed to her and I was frozen in time.

The next day it was time to move everything out of my tiny dorm room and into my new place. I had been working an internship for the majority of my senior year and had gotten a job offer at one of the most prestigious financial consulting firms in New York City. It had been a few months since I and Judi had parted ways amicably and I moved back onto campus. The lust factor was the only thing that had kept us involved. It may have lasted 7 months, tops. After that sizzled out and faded it was time to move on.

Luckily for me, my new career opportunity was footing the bill on a swanky new apartment in Manhattan. It seemed as if it took all day, but after everything was moved in I checked my watch and only six hours had passed. The un-pack was even more tedious. As I took stuff out of boxes I would periodically take breaks; pouring glasses of wine and going out to the balcony terrace to absorb the skyline. Before I knew it, it was six in the morning. Luckily, I didn't have to start work until the following Monday. It was Friday. I spent the next couple of days unpacking and situating things to my liking. I would've enjoyed the weekend if it hadn't blown by so fast.

When Monday came, I awaken to butterflies in my stomach like I was on a first date. As I went through my morning rituals I couldn't seem shake the feeling of anxiety. Once I had completely gotten dressed, I went to pour myself a cup of coffee then lit up a cigarette. One pull of smoke calmly eased my nerves and I began to plateau. Since my apartment was located not too far from my job there wasn't any rush to get to work, but as a reflex I left the house early anyways.

As I strolled down the hallway I couldn't help but notice a stunning blonde lady with a very form fitting dress on. She was fumbling with her suitcase and coffee thermos trying to lock her door. Her beauty had captured my attention so much, that instead of going to the elevator I decided to see if I could be of any assistance.

"Hey, you need help?" I ask.

"Uh, yeah. Thanks. I think I might've tried to do too much at once," she replied. Then she continued, "Are you always this helpful?" she asked after locking her door.

"I try to be when I can," I told her. Then realizing that I was still holding her briefcase I began fumbling for words, "Uh, sorry, here's your stuff," I said as I awkwardly handed back her belongings.

"So, what's your name stranger?" she flatly asked.

"George, and you are?" I asked inquisitively.

"Olivia Sash," she elegantly replied. Then she took a split second to size me up. "So, you don't have a last name? That's odd," she smugly said.

"Oh, it's Sphinx, George Sphinx," I said remembering that I was a trained professional.

"Like the Egyptian statue, right?" she slyly said. Hearing that a lot growing up I just laughed,

"Yeah, exactly," I replied.

When I left my apartment, I had time to kill, but upon checking my watch I quickly realized that I only had twenty minutes to get to work.

"Oh shit, hey Olivia, I don't mean to be rude but I got to go. It was a pleasure meeting you though," I told her. Then I shook her hand and darted down the hallway towards the elevator.

"We live in the same building. I'm sure I'll get more acquainted with her," I thought.

When I got to work, I had about seven minutes to spare. As I strolled through the building, a few people stared at me very curiously. The looks were slightly uncomfortable, but I paid it no mind and continued walking the halls until I found the water cooler. When I reached my destination, my supervisor quickly approached me.

"Hey George, you're early. That's good, I like that. Hey, before you dive into your duties, we're gonna have a meeting in conference room A. just to get everyone acquainted with you and welcome you formally to the company," he said.

"Cool," I said nonchalantly as I filled a paper cup up with water.

"Good, see you in there in five," he replied as he patted my shoulder and walked away. *"Fuck,"* I thought. I hated introductory meetings. They were awkward as hell. Everyone just stares at you, and you have to sit there feeling like a fish squirming out of water. I had experienced this many of times in college.

Once I got to the conference room, I took the nearest seat by the door. As I pretended to fumble with my briefcase, a soft hand touched my shoulder. I swiveled my chair completely around to see who had tapped me, it was Olivia.

"Hey, you work here?" I asked.

"Yeah I do. I was gonna ask you the same question, but that would be dumb considering you're in the same conference room," she said chuckling. The room was filling up fast, and I could feel my anxiety build as the silence settled in.

Once the room was completely quiet, the director began introducing new employees. While he talked, I zoned out. When he got to me, I snapped out of my trance and went through the motions of introducing myself. *"I'm glad that's over,"* I thought once I was finished. The meeting lasted maybe another thirty minutes, and once it was over I quickly shuffled out of the conference room.

"Hey speed racer, my cubicle is next to yours. Wait for me," Olivia said.

"Sure," I replied as I watched her shuffle with her briefcase. As we walked to our desk, Olivia and I made small talk about the company and our expectations of the job ahead of us.

"You know you're like the only black person that works here, right. That doesn't strike you as odd?" she asked once we got to our desk. Up until that point, I hadn't really thought about it.

"What's your point?" I fired back. I could tell that my response had put her on the spot because she quickly began stuttering and trying to find her words.

"I mean, uh, not like that, I mean, you didn't notice? I did. It seemed like while the director was introducing you, everyone was awkwardly staring," she replied. "That shit made *me* kind of uncomfortable," she continued.

"Well, good thing I'm not you. Thanks' for the concerned though," I said smugly. I kind of picked up on that vibe while the meeting was going on, but I quickly disregarded it, not wanting to focus on trivial matters. I studied too hard and too long just to get a job at a prestigious firm to have to focus my energy on miniscule issues. They know I'm black, I know I'm black. If they can't deal with it, that's their problem. Not mine.

As the day seemed to teeter along, I simply lost track of time. It wasn't until Olivia flagged my attention that I stopped what I was doing.

"Hey Georgie boy, you gonna go home? She giggled.

"What?" I asked before checking my watch. It was 6:30. Damn, time really had flown by. As I sat there, I analyzed whether I should stop and go home, or continue working on the report I was almost done with.

"Fuck it, I'll finish at home," I said as I scraped up my papers and quickly stuffed them into my briefcase. Then Olivia walked over to me.

"You wanna go for some sushi?" she softly asked. "I'm hungry as hell, plus it'd be nice to have some company," she continued. I had never eaten sushi before, but I was hungry and she was the only person that had taken a liking to me so I figured why not.

"Sure, you know a place?" I asked.

"Yes, I do. There's this sushi spot near 44th Ave that's really good," she replied with a devilish grin on her face. As we walked to

113

the elevators, a guy that I had noticed staring at me very intensely during the meeting walked up to us.

"Hey Liv, it's me Rodger, from Chap Hall. I thought that was you," he said. For a minute Olivia stalled trying to recall her memory.

"Oh yes, Rod, I mean Rodger. I remember you," she said somberly.

"Yeah, well since we know each other you wanna catch up? I was gonna get some dinner but it seemed only fair I'd invite you," he said arrogantly. Now usually I don't get offended when it seems like a guy is hitting on a woman that I'm not with, but we were heading somewhere together and it seemed like he was blatantly disregarding me, so I decided I'd cut in.

"Uh we're actually going someplace right now Rodger," I said matter of factly.

"Oh, uh cool, yeah. Well maybe another time. Well it was nice seeing you again Liv," he said awkwardly before scurrying away to the stairwell.

"Saved by the bell," Liv said as she took a deep breath and pushed the elevator button. Once we got downstairs the security guard let us out through the security gate and we headed outside.

"You want to catch the train or walk to the spot? She asked. Since I hadn't really seen the night life in downtown Manhattan, I figured a brisk walk would be nice. She agreed, and as we began to walk to the restaurant she held onto my arm.

"You don't mind, do you? She asked timidly.

"Naw, it's cool," I replied.

It took maybe ten minutes or so to arrive at the sushi eatery, but once we got there my stomach was roaring.

As soon as we entered, we hung our jackets up, and found a secluded table located in a pocket of the restaurant. When we sat down the server quickly paced towards our table with menus in hand. He seemed very friendly, though while talking, he was staring us down the whole time. I tried to pay it no mind, as Olivia ordered her meal and then did I. Enjoying the night, we ate, laughed, and talked until the restaurant closed.

"Oh shit! Its 11:30," I said realizing what time it was. *"How could I have lost track time?"* I thought. I had to get up in the morning and finish my report.

"What you worried about? It's not like you live a few blocks away from your job," Olivia said drunkenly.

"You're right," I replied feeling a sigh of relief.

We then paid our checks, grabbed our coats, and exited the restaurant into the downtown fog. Since we both lived in the same building, the trip home was very accompanying. When we made it to our building, the doorman was very friendly and accommodating.

"Good evening sir," he said as he opened the front door. As we entered the building he tipped his hat slightly to show his approval of me being with Olivia. Which I thought was odd, since she wasn't my woman and I had just met her today, but, I was slightly inebriated so I tipped my head in response and kept walking towards the elevator.

Once we made it to our floor, Olivia offered an invite into her apartment,

"Would you like to come inside for a cup of tea?" she asked. The offer was enticing, but I declined.

"I would love to, but I really have to get up early. Maybe next time," I told her.

"You're too nice," she said as she drunkenly leaned in for a hug.

"I try to be," I smoothly replied as I watched her stagger into her unit. After her door shut, I raced down the hall to seek refuge in my humble abode. Once inside, I tossed my suit and briefcase onto the floor and crashed out onto the bed.

When I woke up, I checked my watch and was alarmed to see I had overslept. Having roughly forty minutes to get ready and get to work, I sprang into action. Once I was dressed, I grabbed my briefcase and raced out of the door. After locking my unit, I turned around and was shocked to see Olivia standing right behind me.

"What's up tiger," she said with a smug grin on her face. "I thought you'd be up early Mr. nice guy," she continued. I can't lie, her sarcasm was sexy, so I didn't mind much since I was glad to have some company on the way to work.

"How the hell are you even up early after six shots of Tequila?" I asked.

"Cause that shit was light-weight and I'm a mother-fuckin' vet!" she exclaimed. Since she was 36, I figured she have to be. "*She might be interesting,*" I thought. Her sweet voice and tough demeanor kind of reminded me of Conchita; and for a split second, my mind drifted away as I began thinking of Chi-Chi. I wondered how she was doing in that hell hole.

Chapter 16
The devils lair

It had been a few rough months, but after a while it seemed as if Conchita was settling into her new environment. Since being placed in general population, she had witnessed a stabbing and was even involved in a brawl over a Jell-O cup. The girls on the yard seemed to have taking a liking to her. The lack of showers and disgusting food however, were beginning to take their toll on Conchita's mind. To pass the time, she read at the library most of the hours outside of her cell. When on twenty-three-hour lockdown, she made the best of her time by doing calisthenics. She was determined to not let the shitty food balloon her up like most of the girls there.

Her cell-mate Clarissa wasn't much of a problem either. Clarissa was a heavy set, Hispanic lady in her late forties. She was serving 15 years for her late husband's murder. She claimed he beat her regularly so she stabbed him 27 times with a paring knife. She plead temporary insanity but she was anything but insane, she just managed to fool the prosecutor in her case. She rarely talked much, and mostly just slept and ate. When she wasn't sleeping she would just watch Conchita work out. One day she did speak.

"What are you going to do when you get out?" Clarissa softly asked. Conchita stopped doing push up for a second, sat up and thought about the question for a minute.

"What do you mean? Like for work or what?" Conchita replied seemingly confused about the question.

"Yeah for work," Clarissa said. She didn't even wait for a reply from Conchita before continuing, "I always wonder what I would do once I got out, since I don't have a husband anymore." Not having a response ready, Conchita just looked up at her blankly.

"Fuck! I didn't think about all that," Conchita said as the realization began to set in. She hadn't finished her studies and had no job prospects lined up. The magnitude of the question was starting to weigh in.

"Well, I'll just uh, move in with my Madre' and try to figure things out from there I guess," she told Clarissa.

A few seconds past before the thought of her having to rely on her mother all over again set in. The idea infuriated her so much that it made her snap at Clarissa,

"Just mind your own fuckin' business," Conchita said. Then she turned around and resumed doing push-ups.

The next day while Conchita was in the chow hall, three women approached her while she was eating. The leader, the woman that had slammed the table, was thin and tall and looked like a scare crow. She had a nasty dry scar across her chin. The second one, also thin, was a caramel color with grey eyes. She had features, that by the looks of things, seemed like she might've once been pretty but prison seemed to have taken its toll on her. Now, she was just worn out looking. The last one was fat and short. She was ugly, and looked like she had *never* pretty, not even a little. After scanning the three women, Conchita focused again on the leader. As she assessed the situation at hand, Conchita just sat there quietly and listened to see where the conversation would go.

"Yo bitch, word is you the hoe who kill't my cousin Chacho!" she barked.

After the woman spoke, Conchita just sat there puzzled wondering how she could've known that. She hadn't talked to anyone about her case and she didn't even talk much about herself since being locked up. Her mind was racing a mile a minute and terror was beginning to set in, but now was not the time to talk. Before the woman could say another word, Conchita jumped up, grabbed the tray she was eating from, and smashed the woman in the face with it. The other two women tried to grab Conchita's arms, but she managed to hit the grey eyed one first. She went down like a bag of bricks and was out, but the fat one tackled her to the ground and landed several punches to her nose and eyes. After Conchita was knocked unconscious, the guards quickly rushed to break up the melee. Seeing the guards coming, the fat one quickly got up.

"I didn't do nothing!" the woman yelled as she tried to hide her bloodied hand, but the guards weren't going for it and they handcuffed all three women. Noticing Conchita sprawled out on the floor, they put her on a stretcher and carted her off to the infirmary.

An hour later, Conchita awakened to a bright light beaming into her face. One of her eyes was completely shut and it seemed as if it wouldn't open. As she rubbed her face she began to panicked because it felt like the size of a small pumpkin.

"What the fuck," she said as she sat up. When she turned around, she was startled by the doctor that was silently staring at her.

"Hi Ms. Roseen," he said. "We were worried about you for a minute. You've been unconscious for an hour with a broken nose and an orbital fracture," he continued. After absorbing the news, there was an awkward silence that filled the room.

"Well I'm good now, right?" Conchita asked matter of factly. Upon hearing the question, the doctor looked at her rather peculiar before responding,

"Yes, you're good. Your eye will heal and that broken nose may leave a slight scar, but yeah, you'll be alright," he flatly said. Then he continued, "Now what was that all about?"

"I don't know! Someone hit me from behind and that's all I remember," Conchita barked. She didn't want to slip up and say anything that could escalate the situation and make her stay anymore uncomfortable then it already was. After her response, he blankly stared at her, perplexed because he had been in this situation many of times before. Then he got up, shook his head slowly, and rubbed his brow.

"Suit yourself tough-ass," he said before walking out of the infirmary.

When she got back to her cell, Clarissa was asleep.

"*Of course*," she thought. Sore from earlier, she staggered inside the six by nine cell, flopped onto the top bunk and closed her eyes. "*I wonder what George is doing*," she thought herself before dozing off. Then she began to think of the times when he made her laugh and the first time they made love. As a tear ran down her cheek she slowly started to cry. She sobbed uncontrollably as she felt a sharp pain, like a knife, cut through her chest. The heartbreak was so unbearable that she could hardly breathe. This was the beginning of pain that was to fill her heart for her entire stay.

A week had gone by and Conchita hadn't run into the three women that had beaten her down. One day, while eating, a feeling of relief came over her. "*Things ain't so bad,*" she thought. That feeling was quickly diminished when, while picking through her peas, she saw a tall shadow approaching her. Her eye was still swollen, so it took a moment for her to make out the person standing at the corner of the table. When her vision did clear up, she realized it was the light skinned, gray eyed woman from the brawl.

"Don't worry, I don't want no problems. I just wanted to say sorry," the woman softly said. Conchita stared her up and down. She was poised to respond as she tried to regain her nerves. Her face still hurt, and she was too tired from waking up at the crack of dawn to surge into action. "*Is this a trick? What was this bitch up too?*" Conchita thought.

"Yo, why you sorry huh? That's ya girl you riding with. What you trying' to be cool with me for?" Conchita barked. As she waited for the women to respond, she braced herself with her fist balled tight.

"I'm apologizing because I don't want any problems with you. You get down, and that hook you hit me with let me know you could be problems," the woman told her. "I'll let Chica know to chill. I mean, it *was* her cousin and all, but I knew Chacho, he was always foul. So, I'm sure you had a damn good reason," she continued. As soon as Conchita heard that, she dropped her guard.

"Yo, can I sit down?" the woman asked.

"Yeah, go ahead," Conchita replied. As the thin woman sat down Conchita stared at her intensely waiting for a surprise.

"Yo, I'm Ri-Ri," she said opening a carton of milk. "What's ya name?" she continued.

"I'm Chi-Chi," Conchita said.

"Yo where you learn to hit like that?" Ri-Ri asked.

"I took some Tai Bo exercise classes," Conchita replied. Trying to refrain from spitting out her milk, Ri-Ri turned her head, swallowed and let out a roaring laugh.

"Yo, you dead ass serious? Get the fuck outta here!" Ri-Ri replied. "Yo, my granny had them DVDs. If I knew I could learn that shit, I would've watched the fuck outta em!" she continued. Soon as Ri-Ri finished her sentence they both burst into laughter. While Conchita picked at her food, she and Ri-Ri continued talking and became more acquainted. Turns out, Ri-Ri was from Harlem and was Puerto Rican. Her real name was Rhiandalia Diaz and she was doing time for accessory to arm robbery of a night club where she worked at. Her sentence was fifteen years. So far, she was on year seven. With good time and parole, she would've had a reduction to eleven years, but the fight a week ago didn't help her sentence any.

"So, what're you doing in here? You look like a college girl," Ri-Ri asked.

"Yo I can't talk about it. You know it had some shit to do with Chacho, so I'm not gonna elaborate further," Conchita told her.

"That's peace. I feel you, say no more," Ri-Ri said. As their conversation dwindled, the officers began instructing everyone back to their cells. They quickly gave each other a pound and then rushed off in opposite directions. Every day after that, Conchita and Ri-Ri would meet at their favorite table for lunch and trade stories.

One day while they were chatting, Chica walked up. As soon as she noticed Chica, Conchita began to tense up.

"Yo chill, I ain't here for no problems," Chica hoarsely said. "Ri-Ri asked me to be cool because I don't know all the details. Me and Ruby here," she said pointing to the chubby one, "We just came over to see if we could squash the beef," she continued.

"Yeah we can. Look, what happened to your cousin ain't what the courts made it out to seem like," Conchita explained. "I ain't gonna elaborate on it because my lawyer is working on my appeal, but all I'll say is that I did what I had to do. I never intended for that to happen," she told Chica.

"Okay. Well, we out. Yo Ri-Ri, you coming with us to the yard?" Chica asked.

"Yeah, I'll meet ya'll out there in a few," Ri-Ri hesitantly replied. Before leaving, Chica and Ruby stared her down then turned away to walk towards the exit. Once they were out of sight, Ri-Ri turned to Conchita and said,

"Yo that's my girl and all, but sometimes I don't be wanting to hang with them because they start too much shit out on the yard. Making newbies' find cigarettes for them and shit like that." Then she switched the topic, "but fuck all that, what you gonna do for money when you get out?" she continued. Once again Conchita was confronted with the same question that Clarissa had asked her previously.

"I don't know, honestly," Conchita replied.

"Well you better think fast, because time goes by quick and before you know it, you'll be back out on the streets in no time, and you got less time than me," Ri-Ri said. She knew Ri-Ri was right but it wasn't like she could re-enroll in school and continue her program. Whatever savings her parents did have, went towards her legal defense at her trial. As her mind drifted into deep thought Ri-Ri cut in,

"Yo Chi-Chi you there?" she said waving her hand in front of Conchita's' face.

"Yeah, I was just thinking about something. You're the second person to ask me that shit. To be real, I'm going to be fucked up when I get out," Conchita replied.

"My bad Chi-Chi, I wasn't trying to put too much shit on ya' brain," Ri-Ri said. As the lunch hall roared with chatter, they continued talking for a few more minutes before the guards chimed in and instructed everyone back to their cells. Disappointed, they pounded each other up and headed back to their cages.

As the day's turned into months, and months turned into years, before Conchita knew it, she was on her second year. She had lost her appeal to overturn her case and her conviction was upheld. By this time, her failed appeal didn't even seem to matter much. She had managed to stay out of trouble, keep her shapely figure and even became accustomed to the day to day routine of prison life. Though the food tasted like shit, she became adjusted to it. She even got to enjoy occasional commissary snacks with the money her mother put on her books.

One day while her mother was visiting her, she mentioned that she had run into George days after Conchita's trial. She said she told him where to visit Conchita before she was shipped upstate. He never did. That tid-bit of information infuriated Conchita. *"Why hadn't he come to see me?"* she thought. It was odd though, up until that point she hadn't even thought about him much, and she was almost getting over him.

Though her mother had good intentions, to Conchita, it seemed like she had reopened a wound unknowingly. As they continued talking, Conchita tried to disregard the mention of George. She and her mother conversed for a few more minutes before the guards rudely interrupted their visit.

"Okay Chi-Chi, zip this shit up. It's time for you to go back to your cell," one of the guards barked.

"Hey, there's no reason for that language," her mother said. As Conchita was being cuffed, the guard turned to her mother and replied,

"You're right ma'am. I'm sorry." Conchita's mother accepted his apology, kissed her daughter on the cheek, then departed from the visiting room.

As she sat in her cell all she could think about was why George hadn't come to see her. "*Was he really over me when he messed around with that Judi bitch,*" she thought. As she lay in her bunk she languished over the thought of him not coming to see her before she was sent up.

Later that day, she missed wreck time and even skipped her chats with Ri-Ri. When it was time to eat Clarrisa nudged her shoulder to alert her of meal time.

"Chi-Chi, you going to eat Mami?" Clarissa asked.

"I'm not hungry," Conchita replied.

"Okay, suit yourself," Clarissa said before darting off. Her hunger pains combined with her broken heart were too much to bear. It felt like a giant boulder had fallen onto her. Feeling crushed, she just laid there sobbing, languishing in the pain.

Chapter 17

The devil's demons

The next day had crept up through the night while Conchita cried herself to sleep. When it was time for roll call, she struggled to get out of her bunk. She cried so much during the night that her cheeks were sore and tender from her tears. As she headed to the chow hall she tried to get herself together by pulling her hair into a scraggly ponytail and wiping the sleep out of her eyes. She went through the motions of receiving her food and finding a random place to sit. She was so zoned out that she didn't even look around to see where Ri-Ri was, but as soon as she sat down, Ri-Ri popped up.

"Yo, where were you yesterday?" Ri-Ri asked curiously. The moment she sat down, Conchita felt relieved. She was glad Ri-Ri found her, so she could vent her frustrations to someone.

"I was fucked up man. My Madre' came to visit me yesterday and dropped some news on me. She said that she told my ex where to visit me while I was in holding, but that mother fucker never did. It was bad enough I caught him cheating, but he gone write me off like that and not come see me! What the fuck!" Conchita barked.

"Yo, I know what you mean," Ri-Ri said shaking her head. "My ex testified against me at my trial. I gave him the inside layout of the club and soon as he got caught, he told on me. Mother-fuckers charged me with accessory to robbery," she replied. "These niggas ain't shit," Ri-Ri continued.

"Yep, you right," Conchita said.

"When you get out you should pay that mother fucker back," Ri-Ri said trying to make Conchita feel better. Conchita didn't respond. "*Maybe I should pay him back*, "*But how*?" she thought. By the time

127

she got out, George would probably be way past their relationship. As she zoned out, Ri-Ri snapped her fingers to get her attention.

"Hey girl, you heard me?" Ri-Ri asked.

"Naw, I didn't. What'd you say?" Conchita cluelessly asked.

"I said, if you wanna make some money when you get out, I know a way," Ri-Ri told her.

"How, and doing what?" Conchita asked.

"Well, since you sexy and all, I know a woman name Frieda that runs an underground escort service. She knows business men, high rollers, and ballers. That's what I did part time while I worked at the club. That's also where I met my scumbag ex-boyfriend," she said reminiscing. "Hey, maybe when I get out I can show you the ropes. If you ain't pussy," she continued.

"I'm down," Conchita replied.

Shocked that it took no convincing, Ri-Ri just stared at her for a second.

"Uh, okay. Im'a have my sister rummage through my shit to try to find the number for me. In the meantime, gimme' a number to reach you at, so when I'm out we can link back up," she said. After writing down her mother's phone number they resumed talking about lighter things. As soon as Ri-Ri began telling her escorting stories, it was time to head back to their cell.

"Awe fuck, I hate that shit. You know when you telling a good story, and then you gotta finish it later. I hate this fuckin' place," Ri-Ri growled. After giving each other a pound, they returned to their cells.

The following day, Conchita seemed to be feeling much better and while in the library, she discovered some pamphlets about an early release program. It stated, that for every 2 credits an inmate receive, they'd get 6 months shaved off their sentence. When it was lunch time, she raced to the chow hall to find Ri-Ri so she could share the news.

Upon entering the hall, she noticed that there were only a few people there. In the meantime, she grabbed a tray and went through the motions in line. After receiving her food, she copped a squat at the nearest table where she could get a clear view of people entering the hall. As the lunch room filled up, she began digging at her mash potatoes, and then, not a moment too soon, Ri-Ri entered the hall.

"Hey yo, Ri-Ri," Conchita said yelling through the hall's noisy atmosphere. After filling her tray, Ri-Ri raced towards Conchita and sat down.

"Yo, what's good? You all hype today and shit," Ri-Ri said.

"Yo, I know how you can get out of here a few years early," Conchita blurted out. Shocked, Ri-Ri just stared at her before replying,

"Yo don't be fucking with me. Since I been here they done denied my parole three times. I've been in four fights, so I'm pretty sure I'm gonna have to do the max of my time," she said broken spirited.

"No seriously, if you take these classes they knock off six months for every two credits you get. Take the classes with me and I'll help you. You could be out a little bit after I get out," Conchita said sliding the pamphlet to Ri-Ri.

"Okay I'm game," Ri-Ri said after looking it over. Then they began talking about what they were going to do once they were released. They babbled on until chow time was up, and when it was, once again, they pounded each other up and headed to their cells.

When the first day of class finally came, they found their desks and sat next to each other. They had class every day before lunch time. Conchita had been to school before so it was nothing to her, but Ri-Ri hadn't even finished high school, so staying awake posed more of a challenge to her then the class work. Every time Ri-Ri dozed off, Conchita nudged her before the teacher had a chance to catch her sleeping. Ri-Ri didn't even respond, she'd just re-adjust herself in her desk and look alert. After class, Conchita chewed Ri-Ri up like a disappointed mother.

"Yo, you got to stay awake. Come on man, at least try. Yo ass is full of energy anytime else, why you dozing off in class?" she barked.

"Because school is boring as fuck girl. That's why I dropped out," Ri-Ri replied.

"Well look, you have to ask yourself one thing; how bad you wanna get out this mother fucker," Conchita barked.

"Real bad," Ri-Ri told her.

"Well then act like it," Conchita replied.

"You right," Ri-Ri said.

After the brief lecture, they then headed to the library to study for a half an hour.

While taking her classes, Conchita had finalized a plan for when she was released. She would get a bullshit job until she linked back up with Ri-Ri, work the escorting business, then she would find George for revenge. He was not about to cheat on and abandon her at her most vulnerable moment in life and get away with it.

Chapter 18:
Worlds away from hell

Two years had fallen off the calendar when suddenly I realized things were going perfect. I had a great job, a nice apartment and I and Liv had developed into a, *'friends with benefits'* type of relationship. She was career driven and very ambitious, as I was, so it fit perfectly. We would work during the week then link up for the weekend for a little R&R. I'd have to admit; the sex was great too. She did every nasty thing imaginable. She liked rough sex too, sort of like Conchita, but less sensual. She was also very frisky. While at work, she would sneak into the unisex bathroom with me for a little quickie, to which I would oblige.

One day while trying to sneak in a quickie, someone entered the bathroom. Feeling panic set in, we froze in the stall waiting for whoever it was to finish. Once they were done, we resumed our little soiree'. After we finished, I grabbed her by the arm and scolded her,

"Hey you gotta chill. I like what we do but we're gonna get fired," I said. Not taking me seriously, she paused for a second before replying,

"Relax, Georgie boy. You worry too much," she said as she strolled down the hall. **This would become a daily occurrence.**

A few weeks later, as I was walking down the hallway, I noticed that asshole Rodger blocking Liv's path as she tried to go back to her cubicle. Now we weren't dating or nothing like that, but I didn't like to see any woman that I was cool with being harassed. It looked like he was trying to 'Mack' to her but she wasn't having it. As I stood there watching, they didn't even seem to notice me. To make sure I didn't jump the gun, I stood down the hall and listened.

"Look Rodger, I'm not into you like that no more," Liv said.

"C'mon Liv, we had a good thing going on back in college," Rodger snapped. "What? Is it that nigger you're always around? Are ya'll fucking or something Liv?" he continued. When he said that, Liv's eyes grew wide,

"That is not acceptable Rodger. He is a human being! Not a nigger, you racist son of a bitch!" she fired back. At that point, I felt the need to intervene.

"Yo Rodger, she said beat it," I said as I firmly placed my hand on his shoulder. Surprised that I was standing behind him, his face turned pale white like he had seen a ghost.

"I, I, I," he said as he stumbled over his words. He quickly dropped his arm from Liv's path and nervously rushed down the hall.

"Look at you. My black Clark Kent," Liv said as she leaned in close.

"Well, you looked like you could use some rescuing," I said chuckling. As I laughed, she laid her head on my chest and hugged me tight.

"Georgie boy, I could get used to this," she said as she nestled her head. I could tell that she was starting to become more emotionally invested in me. Not sure what to do, I continued to rub her head,

"Hey let's get back to work," I said. We quickly broke away from our interlock and trotted back down the hall to our cubicles.

After work, we agreed to go to our favorite sushi place and have a couple of drinks. While Liv was wrapping up her reports, I grabbed my coat and got up with the intentions of finding Rodger.

"Hey, I've got to handle something," I told her. Preoccupied, she nodded and continued riffling through her papers. Once I was out of sight, I walked through the halls in search of Rodger.

Because of Liv, I didn't get to say to him what I really wanted to earlier. As I continued walking through the corridors of the office, I couldn't seem to find him anywhere. Just as I was making my way back to my desk, there he was, going towards the break room. As he walked inside, I followed in behind him. Once we were both in the room, I quickly collared him up.

"I didn't want to say it earlier because I didn't want to cause a scene in front of Liv, but if you ever call me a nigger again, I'm gonna' to fuck you up. You got it?" I said as I tightened my grip on his collar.

"Yeah man. I'm sorry. I didn't mean that, man," he said visibly shaken with fear.

"Fuck being sorry. Don't let it happen again. Oh, and if you mention this shit to anyone, I'll have Liv back me up about your little racial epithet," I snarled. Then I loosened my grip and stared him down.

"That's what I thought," I said as I walked out of the breakroom. Upon returning to my cubicle, I noticed Liv was ready to go.

"Where'd you go to?" she curiously asked.

"I had to use the bathroom real quick," I said. I was lying. I just didn't want her to know about my confrontation with Rodger.

"Well, just for that record, that wasn't *really quick*. You were gone fifteen minutes. What you'd have to do, take a number two?" she said giggling.

"No, but you know, sometimes it takes a minute to wrap up the elephant trunk," I said ushering her towards the elevator. As we waited for the doors to open, we both began laughing hysterically before stepping inside.

Once we got to the sushi spot we began ordering every sushi dish on the menu; at $3 a plate, why not. We ordered dozens of shots;

laughed about the office meetings, Rodger's stupid ass and the bullshit catering the office ordered every other Friday. She was beginning to grow on me, but I wasn't ready to take it there with her so I dismissed the thought and continued enjoying the evening.

When I woke up the next day, I could still taste the patron' on my breath. We ended up at my place. Upon opening my eyes, I noticed Liv was missing, but before I could get up I instantly realized where she was. She was between my legs sucking my dick. Now this was a good morning. She was working her lips on me like a surgeon delicately removing an organ. It took six minutes, maybe seven, before I exploded right into her mouth. I couldn't see her but I could feel her licking everywhere below my waist. This woman was amazing. After finishing, she slid between my legs and popped her head up from beneath the covers.

"Hey tiger," she said with bourbon still on her breath. Her voice was hoarse from drinking and chain smoking all night. It was sexy though. "I see you're awake now," she continued. As I lay there floating on cloud nine, it took a few seconds to form a thought,

"Hell yeah," I said wiping the sleep from my eyes. Before I could get my cigarettes, Liv reached over, lit one up, and handed it to me.

"Are you hungry?" she asked,

"Yeah, I could do for a nice breakfast," I replied. Immediately she popped out of the bed and darted for the kitchen. As the aroma filled the air, I lay there taking in deep puffs of my cigarette. The euphoria was filling my body. This was becoming a beautiful start to whatever she and I were doing.

After four years, Liv and I were now an item. She was a good woman. My professional life was also going well. I was doing such a tremendous job at work that I received several promotions and raises. With the pay increase and bonuses, I even upgraded my penthouse apartment. It was so sleek that Liv periodically talked about moving in together, but we hadn't officially agreed on that move. She ended up getting a job at another firm and I was climbing the corporate ladder at my job. Life was good. The days were long but the money was well worth it. Then as time winded on, things with Liv and I became routine and boring. Our outings after work for sushi and drinks were replaced with ballroom dinners and hors d'oeuvres. My mind was beginning to turn into mush. It wasn't too bad but I needed some excitement.

Then one day as I was jogging down the street, I was suddenly stopped in my tracks. At first, I thought was I seeing a mirage', but as I got closer I was dumbfounded by what I saw. It was Conchita. She was out. Up until that point I hadn't even notice how fast the time had flown by. She looked good too. She had the same shape and her face still looked fresh. As I stared her, she didn't even seem to notice me as she was too busy taking orders. My first thought was to turn in the opposite direction and keep jogging, but then I thought, *"If she works here it'll be a matter of time before we cross paths,"* so I made my way towards the cafe'. When I got inside, I quickly took a seat at a nearby booth and pretended to look at a menu. Once she got to my table, she instantly froze in her tracks.

"Hey, uh, what can I get you," she struggled to conjure up.

"Hi Chi-Chi," I smoothly said. I could tell she was shocked to see me and it seemed as if I had thrown her rhythm completely off.

"George. What are you doing in this area?" she asked.

"I live in this area now," I replied.

"You must have a good job then? Huh?" she coldly said.

"You could say that," I replied. "Look I'm sorry how things ended between us, I really am. I didn't mean to hurt you," I continued.

"Well it doesn't matter now. I'm out, and that's in the past," she said harshly. Before she could continue, she was flagged down by another patron. "Look if you need more time to order, look at the menu," she said sharply. I wasn't really hungry but I was extremely surprise to see her, so I figured I'd order something just to keep talking to her. It was clear though that she was jaded by me and how we had broken up. As I sat there scanning the menu I began feeling like a dick head. My mind was telling me to get up and leave, but as soon as I made the attempt to, she had returned to take my order.

"So, what are you getting?" she flatly asked.

"I'll get the Rangoon dish," I said. As soon as I placed my order she quickly grabbed the menu and walked away.

"Hey, Chi-Chi, c'mon don't be like that," I pleaded.

"What do you mean, don't be like that? Be like what? You didn't even come to see me while I was in the county. You cheated on me then left me out to dry. I loved you. Before all that shit happened with my brother I devoted time to your stupid ass! Some shit comes up with my family and you instantly feel abandoned. Lonely enough to fuck another bitch and abandon me!" she snarled. "Fuck you nigga!" she continued. When she said that, I had nothing, no comeback, no nothing, but she wasn't finished.

"And to make things worse, you didn't even come to the funeral. You thought I didn't notice, but I did. Now, I have to work. If you need anything else, I'll send Cindy over to your table," she shrewdly said. After she walked away I wanted to cry. Everything she said was true.

As I sat there teetering the thoughts in my head, the other server Cindy, brought out my food. I sat there poking at my meal and drifting into deep thought as I gazed at Conchita. The whole time I stared at her, she might've looked over at me maybe once and that was to cut her eyes. My server Cindy was very pleasant but I didn't come in for her, hell, I didn't even come in for the food. I came in to settle things with Conchita and at least bury the hatchet, but she was hell bent on hating me. So, I paid for my meal and quietly left. My heart felt like it had dropped in my shoe as I walked out of the café'. I wasn't gonna give up that easy though. As soon as she got off of work I would try to reprise the issue.

"Damn," Conchita said once she was inside the break room. She had intended on looking for George when she got all her ducks in a row, but this surprise encounter had completely caught her off guard. *"I'll just spin him for now and hook him in later,"* she thought. She could tell by the look in his eyes that he wasn't completely over her. Once she contained the racing thoughts in her head, she quickly proceeded back to work.

After going through the motions of mechanically taking orders, her shift seemed to have ended quickly. She counted the money she made the restaurant along with her tips, then she jetted for the door. Once she was outside, George popped up from around the corner.

"Conchita," he said. As he got closer she pretended to be mad by putting on a scowled look.

"Aw shit," she said.

"Look, I know I fucked up but I just want you to know, I did love you. I still do. I just felt like you weren't into me anymore, aside from the issue with your brother," he told her. "And I'm sorry for not

137

making his funeral," he continued. Trying not to be a complete bitch, she broke her stone-cold demeanor,

"Okay, okay. I forgive you," she said. When George heard that he cracked a gigantic smile.

"Yo, so when did you get out?" he asked.

"Like three or four months ago," she said.

"I thought you were sentenced to six years. How'd you get out so soon," he curiously asked.

"Why? You wanted me to stay locked up?" she replied. She enjoyed seeing him squirm.

"No, not like that, I just remember what your mother told me is all," he told her.

"I'm joking," she said giggling. "I took some classes and kept out of trouble so they released me early," she explained.

"That's what's up. So, I guess you can tell me why you got locked up in the first place now," he asked.

"Yeah, I can tell you *now*, but we gotta walk and talk though. I hate getting home late," she replied. As they traded stories about how drastic their lives had turned out, she never did get around to telling him why she was locked up.

When they reached her mothers' house, he asked for her number but Conchita told him she didn't have a cell phone yet. Not wanting to lose touch with him, she told him to drop by the café, on the days she was working. George agreed, and then took off in the opposite direction heading home. As Conchita stood on the steps, a small part of her was happy to see him, but a much larger part of her was still jaded. The thoughts race in her mind like a hurricane whirling around a deserted island. Still in a dazed, she turned around to walk up the Brownstown steps.

Once inside, her mother greeted her and hung up her jacket. She then proceeded to serve Conchita a plate from the meal she had prepared. Before Conchita could even share the news about her run in with George, her mother told her that a woman named Ri-Ri had called.

"She said to call her as soon as possible," her mother said.

"Thanks Madre', I'll call her tomorrow," Conchita replied taking the piece of paper her mother handed her. Ri-Ri never did find Frieda's number before Conchita left prison. She then continued to eat her meal and chat with her mother for the rest of the evening. She left out the fact that she had run into George earlier that day. After she finished her meal she dumped her plate into the sink, kissed her mother on the cheek, and headed to her room. As she changed into her night gown, she thought about George for the rest of the evening until she closed her eyes and drifted off to sleep.

When I got back home I didn't even bother calling Liv. I was so excited about running into Conchita that I didn't think about anything else. Funny thing though, I hadn't thought about Conchita much in the four and a half years that had snook up on me, but seeing her tonight brought back every emotion I ever had. Not to mention she looked very beautiful, even in her server smock. Other than the slight scar on the side of her eye, her appearance was virtually the same.

Black Devil-Blue Eyes

Chapter 19
The beginning of devilish deeds

When Conchita woke up the next day she immediately called Ri-Ri. She was so much in a rush that she didn't even bother brushing her teeth before calling. Ri-Ri was so excited to hear from her that she began screaming upon recognizing Conchita's voice. She had been celebrating all of the four days since her release.

"Hey ba-by," Ri-Ri's voice boomed through the receiver.

"Yo where the fuck you at?" Conchita asked.

"I'm at my people's place mother fucker!" Ri-Ri replied. The noise was blaring so loud it sounded like Ri-Ri was at a night club. Too much for Conchita to stand at eight in the morning, she yelled into the phone,

"Yo, just hit me up when you settle down," she told Ri-Ri.

Ri-Ri agreed and Conchita hung up the phone. She then laid back down and stared at the ceiling trying go back to sleep. Unable to, she jumped up to hit the shower. After freshening up and getting some breakfast into her system, Conchita sat down on the couch and waited for Ri-Ri to call back. While waiting for the call, she began to doze off, when all of a sudden, not a minute too soon, the phone rang.

"Hey bitch, wake yo ass up," Ri-Ri screeched into the phone.

"I'm woke, shit. What's up, where you at?" Conchita asked.

"I'm on Lenox and 144th, right now, but look, im'a meet you on your side in like 45 minutes. What's your address?" Ri-Ri rattled off.

Conchita gave her the address, and then hung up the phone. Soon after, she drifted back to sleep. Ri-Ri must've been excellent with time because she was at Conchita's door exactly within 45 minutes. Startled from the banging at the door, Conchita hopped up to quickly answer it. When she opened the door, Ri-Ri was standing there cheesing like a cheesy cat.

"Damn girl, you one noisy mother fucker. I see why ya ass got locked up! Come in," Conchita snapped. When Ri-Ri stepped inside she asked for something to drink. Conchita reluctantly obliged, but went to fetch some orange juice from the fridge.

"So, what's good? You got Frieda's' number?" Conchita asked when she returned.

"Yo my bad, I'm just so glad to see you. Look, I'm sorry I didn't get you Frieda's' number before you left the box. I don't have her number with me now either, but I know where her spot is," Ri-Ri explained.

"So, let's go," Conchita replied.

"Yo slow down. Frieda don't even get up until 2, so you gonna have to just chill. It ain't gonna even take thirty minutes to get there from here. So, look, let's roll up. Get relaxed and shit. You got me to focus in that class and shit, and I thank you for that, but now im'a get you focused for this shit," Ri-Ri said. Seeing the impatience in Conchita's face, Ri-Ri continued, "I know you hyped and shit," she said as she licked her phillie blunt. Disappointed, Conchita just sat back staring at Ri-Ri while she filled her blunt with weed.

As they smoked and laughed about their jail house stories, Conchita noticed that it was nearly 1:45.

"Oh shit girl, it's damn near two o'clock. We gotta go," Conchita abruptly said.

"It's okay girl. It ain't like it's a job interview, the later the better," Ri-Ri replied. Then they quickly grabbed their jackets and left the house.

When they arrived at Frieda's, Conchita grew suspicious as she surveyed the shabby house.

"Yo, she got high roller clientele?" Conchita asked perplexed.

"Don't trip. She likes to be low-key. I guess she doesn't want to draw attention to herself," Ri-Ri said. After hearing that, Conchita felt at ease and they made their way up the steps. When they knocked on the door, a few minutes went by and no one answered.

"Come on girl let's go," Conchita said.

"Yo, are you trying to get this money or not?" Ri-Ri asked sternly. Not wanting Ri-Ri to think she was scared, she kept quiet and waited.

Growing impatient Ri-Ri knocked again; this time louder. When the door finally opened a slender brown skin woman in her fifties answered. Frieda was at least six feet tall and stood like a giant in the door way.

"Bitch I heard you the first time," she said elegantly. She had the features of a Diana Ross and a booming voice similar to Patty LaBelle's. Frieda also wasn't shy as she answered the door wearing only a negligée'.

"Ya bitches come inside. Ya'll making' my mutha' fuckin' house cold. Standing there looking like two stray cats," she commanded. When they entered the house, Conchita looked around and noticed that everything was white. From the marble floors to the curtains, everything was bright white. There was even a glass statue of a white Great Dane, in the middle of the living room floor.

"What's up with the dog statue?" Conchita asked.

"Because men are dogs but they're beautiful. I don't know bitch, it was a fly ass statue, make up your own meaning of it," Frieda quipped.

When they got to the living room, she ordered them to sit down on a long white couch.

"First off, you're gonna need sexier threads. Ya'll look like some jailhouse bitches, cute bitches, but jail house bitches no less. Especially you," she said pointing to Ri-Ri. She then took both women into another room and told them to pick out some clothes. Both Conchita and Ri-Ri ransacked the enormous closet like children in a candy shop. Before allowing them to put on anything she commanded them to take showers.

After they were done, Frieda sat them down and began explaining how they should conduct themselves while working for her. Since Ri-Ri had been through this screening before, most of Frieda's' run down was directed towards Conchita. When she finished, she gave them an address and told them not to be late. They agreed, then immediately left her presence.

Once they were outside Conchita turned to Ri-Ri and began questioning her,

"Damn girl, she's mad' strict. Are we really gonna make some money though?" she asked. Slowly opening a sucker, Ri-Ri just looked at Conchita,

"Yes girl, yes. We're gonna' get this gwalla' okay, sheesh! You just better be ready when we go to meet up with these trick-ass mother-fuckers tonight," she replied. Obediently listening, Conchita didn't say anything back, she just nodded. Then they began making their way up the street.

When the time had arrived, butterflies were floating around in Conchita's stomach like crazy. Her anxiety was at full level until they got to the Chateau la Luxor, a high-end hotel. To help ease Conchita's nerves, Ri-Ri took out a joint and told her to lite up.

After taking a few puffs, they then headed inside the hotel to entertain their guest. Upon arriving in the lobby, Ri-Ri nudged Conchita's arm,

"Hey look, there they go," she said pointing towards two large white men. They looked about fiftyish and they had to be either body builders or mob guys because they looked tough. Clean cut, but tough. Once they approached the men they greeted themselves and sat at a vacant booth.

When the men began talking, they spoke with thick European accents. While talking about themselves, they made sure to be very brief and very vague about what they did. When the server arrived, the men ordered for themselves and for both of the women. Conchita and Ri-Ri didn't mind much, since the men *were* paying for everything. As they enjoyed the night, they parlayed the evening drinking, eating, and laughing. Once they had finished the last bottle, one of the gentlemen leaned toward Conchita,

"We'd like you both to come to our room and show us a sexier side of yourselves," he whispered. Even though Conchita was thoroughly drunk, her butterflies had returned in full affect.

"Sure, okay," she said trying not to appear nervous. When Conchita got up from the booth, Ri-Ri put her arm across her shoulder,

"Don't worry, Mami. Relax baby, I gotchu," she said softly kissing Conchita on the lips. At first Conchita was confused about the kiss, but Ri-Ri's words seemed to have put her at ease.

As they departed from the table the men dropped wads of cash onto the disarrayed mess, then headed to their suite with Conchita and Ri-Ri in tow.

Once inside the suite, the men instructed both women to strip naked and join them in the shower. The men must've been well paid because the room was decked out with many amenities. Conchita was wowed. As soon as both women were in the shower, Conchita let the water drench her body and went with the flow. As the water poured over her, Ri-Ri kissed her some more while both men began pleasuring them.

Afterwards, they re-entered the master suite and one of the men took out an envelope and tossed it to them.

"It's six thousand dollars in there," he said as he poured a drink into a shiny crystal glass. Both women stared inside the envelope as the man took a sip, watching them pensively.

"We can do this once a month. We'll call Frieda when we're in town. Oh, and you girls were great," he told them. As he spoke, they nodded their heads pretending to listen while they counted the money. They then divvied up the cash, got dress and exited the hotel room. Since she was too drunk to make it to her side of town, Conchita decided to crash at Ri-Ri's mother's apartment.

Once they got there, they agreed to wake up at six in the morning before making their way to Frieda's. This would be the beginning of something exciting and wild for Conchita. When the morning arrived, they went to Frieda's house, dropped off her cut, and received more contacts before leaving.

The next day, after sleeping in, Conchita realized that she hadn't picked up her last paycheck at the café'. It wasn't like she needed the money, considering she had just made $2250 the night before, but all money was good money. So, she jumped up and sprang into motion.

After freshening up she darted for the door. When she got outside, Ri-Ri was already standing there on the porch about to knock.

"Ri-Ri, what the fuck you doing here?" Conchita asked.

"Frieda called me and wanted to see if we could do a date tonight. Spur of the moment type shit," she said. "I would've called you but I was already out, so I said fuck it and came over," she continued. Ri-Ri was so rough around the edges. When they went on their dates, she rarely spoke. Since Conchita was the one that could pull off being soft spoken, she did all the talking.

"Yeah what time?" Conchita asked.

"Like ten tonight," Ri-Ri replied. "Where were you headed?" she then curiously asked.

"To get my last check from the café'. I almost forgot about it," Conchita replied.

"I know you *did*, with all the bread we just made. I would've forgotten about that bullshit-ass check too!" Ri-Ri said laughing hysterically. Then Conchita locked the door and both women took off.

When they arrived at the café, Conchita quickly went to the back of the restaurant to get her check from the manager. Angry that she hadn't showed up for her shift he tried questioning her, but she wasn't having it. She snatched her check, flipped him the bird and told him she quit. When she exited the cafe, she was shocked to see George standing out front. She had forgotten she told him to drop by the café if ever he wanted to see her.

"George, uh, hey," she said stumbling over her words.

"I was nearby, so figured I'd check you out. You've been on my mind a lot lately and I didn't have to work today, so," he said matter of factly.

"Well you're lucky, I just quit. If you had come by later I wouldn't have been here," she replied.

"Well what you gonna do for work," he asked.

"I've got some things lined up," Conchita told him. Then as they continued conversing, Ri-Ri interrupted,

"Ooh, who's he? He's cute; you freelancing Chi-Chi?" Ri-Ri asked.

"Freelancing?" George asked sounding confused.

"Don't mind her. She say's dumb shit a lot," Conchita said pushing Ri-Ri away. While they chatted, Ri-Ri stood in the background like a lost puppy. Growing tired of lingering in the distance, Ri-Ri snapped,

"Yo, I'm out. Meet me at the spot tonight," she said with an attitude before storming off. Paying Ri-Ri no mind, Conchita nodded and continued talking with George as they strolled down the street.

While they talked, she disclosed what had transpired that led to her being arrested. Everything that is, except the fact that *she* had killed Chacho. She put that off on her cousin Roberto. Knowing that she had a violent streak, George was completely un-phased by her story. He just listened.

As they walked and talked, several hours had burned by. When Conchita realized this, she kissed George on his cheek and started to race off to catch the nearest train. Before she could take flight he softly grabbed her arm,

"Here take my number," he said placing a piece of paper in her hand. He then offered to go with her but she declined his request and took off running.

As the train raced through the tunnel like a bullet, Conchita's mind was in disarray with thoughts. What if they continued their previous relationship; how would she tell him her new profession; and what if he betrayed her again. It was then and there that she decided that she was not going to give a full 100% of herself to him again. If anyone got hurt, it wouldn't be her. This time she would play it from the outside; methodically watching him and focusing her attention on making money. When she got home, she quickly began getting ready for another eventful night.

Chapter 20:
Demons and mischief

Later that evening when Conchita got to her destination, Ri-Ri was nowhere in sight. *"What the fuck. How's this bitch gonna be late?"* she thought. Conchita wasn't as confident without Ri-Ri and her butterflies were beginning to race. To relieve her anxiety, she lit up a cigarette and took a deep pull. Before she could finish, Ri-Ri suddenly popped up.

"Hey bitch!" she said ecstatically. Startled by how Ri-Ri had snuck up behind her, Conchita dropped her cigarette.

"Yo, don't fuckin' do that shit. You scared the shit out of me. My nerves are already bad! I thought you were gonna' leave me hanging to do this shit alone," Conchita snapped.

"Now you know I wouldn't do that to you, Chica," Ri-Ri said holding back her laugh. Comforted by that notion, Conchita felt at ease and they quickly went inside the hotel. As they walked through the lobby, Ri-Ri unzipped her purse slightly and nudged Conchita,

"Look what I got," she said showing Conchita a silver .38 snub nose pistol.

"What you doing with that? I thought we were dealing with high class men. Why do you need that?" Conchita asked.

"Just in case mami, just in case," Ri-Ri replied with a smirk on her face.

As they continued through the lobby trying to locate their clients, Ri-Ri spotted them. Conchita was instantly disgusted at the sight of the second man. Both men were fat, but the second man was morbidly obese. When they got close up on them, Conchita could smell an odor permeating from his body. Though he was disgustingly smelly, the women went through the motions like any other date. By the end of the night, the men were desperately trying to get both women upstairs for sex. After enduring the rank smell all night both women struggled to go upstairs, but reluctantly did so for the sake of the money.

Once they were in the room, the men began pouring more champagne' and disrobing. Conchita decided to stall them by slipping into the bathroom while Ri-Ri stayed behind on the couch. While in the bathroom she tried to muster up the courage to go through with it; but when she returned the obese man was on top of Ri-Ri plowing away at her. From the look on Ri-Ri's face she seemed to not like how the soirée' was going at all. The other man wasn't even engaging sexually, he was just sitting at the end of the couch with his hands around her throat.

Shocked, Conchita just stood there frozen in the middle of the room. As Ri-Ri's face was turning blue, she didn't even try to get the man's hands from around her neck. Instead she fumbled for her purse at the bottom of the couch searching for her pistol. Once she had it, she cocked the hammer back and pointed it at the man choking her. Seeing the gun, he immediately let go of her neck and tried to grab her hands, but she managed to fire off a round, shooting him square in the wrist.

"Awwwwww," he shrilled as blood rushed out of his arm. The man fucking her, hopped up and tried to flop behind the couch but he was too slow. Ri-Ri lurched up like a swift ally cat and pistol whipped him across the head, knocking him out cold. She then turned her attention back to the man she shot, and held the pistol to his head.

"Where's the money?" she asked breathing heavily.

"It's in the duffle bag in the room," he said trying to control his bleeding wrist. She then turned to Conchita,

"If he moves, shoot em'," Ri-Ri said with the pistol still on him. Then she quickly forced Conchita to take the gun as she ran into the room in search of the money. It must've taken Ri-Ri a split second to retrieve the bag because she was back in a flash.

When she returned, she angrily snatched the pistol away from Conchita. After quickly getting dress, she walked back up to the wounded man, while he was still groaning, and smacked him in the head with the pistol. Then she turned to Conchita,

"Chi-Chi, snap the fuck out of it. We gotta jet. Grab ya' shit," she barked. Without hesitation, Conchita obediently complied and they frantically left the room.

Once they were in the hallway, they could hear police radios in the distance. Thinking quick on their toes, they raced towards the emergency stairwell to evade the cops. When they got outside, they found themselves standing behind the hotel in a vacant lot. Still pissed, Ri-Ri began berating Conchita.

"Why the fuck did you just stand there when you saw him chocking the shit outta' me?" she asked.

"I was shocked. That shit looked gross as fuck, with that fat mother fucker on top of you sweating. I thought you were into that choking shit. I couldn't tell," Conchita replied,

When she said that Ri-Ri stared at her for few seconds, then they both burst hysterically into laughter.

"You're a funny bitch, but I fucks' with you. And see," holding up the gun, "I told you just in case," she said with an evil grin on her face. They then quickly scurried through the parking lot, and as they weaved between cars, watched as several police officers entered inside the hotel.

After quickly making their way off the property and down a side street, they called a cab. Feeling paranoid that the police might find them, they spotted a local bar and ducked inside as they waited for their taxi to arrive. While sitting at a booth, Ri-Ri shuffled through the duffle bag scanning the bills inside.

"Girl it looks like about ten stacks in here," Ri-Ri said. "They must've wanted to do some freaky ass shit, and Frieda didn't even bother to mention that they were some weirdo's," she continued.

"Yeah about Frieda, what are we gonna tell her?" Conchita asked with a worried look on her face. After considering the question, Ri-Ri just stared at Conchita before answering,

"We gonna' tell her that that freaky ass mother fucker tried to strangle me to death, and that I shot him in self-defense. He ain't dead, so don't worry. I got this," she said. As soon as Ri-Ri said that, the taxi cab pulled up and they bolted out of the bar and into the night.

Ri-Ri knew that Frieda hated unnecessary drama, so when they got to her house, she wasn't surprised at all. From the time she opened the door; to when they sat down in her living room, Frieda was going off. When she stopped, that's when Ri-Ri interjected,

"Um, the mother fucker was chocking me, and I couldn't breathe," she said casually. Still riled up, Frieda looked at her briefly,

"Bitch, I don't care if he killed you! You better hope that mother fucker doesn't send the cops around here. I know that much. If the cops come around here looking for you, ima' kill yo ass myself," she yelled. Then she continued "Look, ya hoe's gonna have to lay-low until all this shit blows over. Gimme' a month or so, and if the cops don't come sniffing around, I'll resume giving ya'll appointments. Now get," she said snapping her fingers. Not wanting to piss her off further, both women did as they were told and quickly darted for the door.

Once they were outside, Conchita grabbed Ri-Ri's arm,

"Yo, a month? What the fuck we gonna' do until then?" she asked. Clueless, Ri-Ri stopped walking as she tried to think of an answer.

"You got some money saved up, right? That should last you until we get back rolling," she replied. Ri-Ri was right; they had clocked about $7,000 a piece in the last couple of dates they had been on, so they would be fine. Only problem now, was that Conchita would have to leave the house in the evenings so as not to cause her mother to become suspicious. If her mother noticed her at home more often she would start questioning her. She didn't want that. As they stood on the curb pondering ideas, the rain began coming down harshly. Wanting to escape the rain, they decided to go to Ri-Ri's house so they could get their thoughts together. Ri-Ri was generous like that. She treated Conchita like a sister.

While they sat in Ri-Ri's living room bouncing ideas back and forth, Conchita decided to call George. It rang several times, with no answer, before going to voicemail. *"Maybe he's at work,"* she thought. After a few more attempts, she gave up and went back to focusing on Ri-Ri's rambling. Hours went by while they sat in the living room smoking joints and reminiscing about the events that had unfolded earlier. As time winded along, Conchita became exhausted and drifted off to sleep. After several hours had passed, her slumber was cut short and she was awakened by the ringing of her phone.

"Hello," she groggily answered.

"Chi-Chi?" said the voice on the other end. It was George. Happy to hear his voice, Conchita immediately sat up.

"George, hey Papi," she said trying to sound alert.

"I see you called me earlier. I was busy doing some paperwork, what's up," he replied. While they chatted, she mentioned that she had loss her 'new job'. Feeling sorry for her, he offered to meet up to see if he could help. Relieved, Conchita agreed then hung up. Soon afterwards, she sprang into action to freshen up. Once she was put together, she then headed for the door. Not wanting to wake up Ri-Ri she locked the door from the inside and jetted off.

It took about forty-five minutes to reach him, but once she did he was already there. When she walked up, he pulled her close and kissed her softly on the lips.

"Hey mami, you look beautiful," he quietly said. That made her smile from ear to ear. He was always sweet like that. They then tried to figure out what restaurant to eat at, and once they did, began making their way there.

Once they got to the restaurant, he went through the motions of taking her coat and pulling out her seat. When their server arrived, they ordered and continued talking.

"So, are you seeing anyone?" Conchita asked.

"Yeah, sort of. We've been dating a few, but it's nothing serious," he replied. "I mean, she wants to move in but we haven't agreed to that yet. Hopefully it doesn't come up again," he continued. The sound of him talking about another woman infuriated Conchita. It was at that moment she realized that one woman could never really captivated his attention enough to keep him. Broken hearted, she pretended not to be bothered and continued listening to him.

"So, what's happening with your job situation," he abruptly asked. Forgetting that she had told him about her job, she struggled to come up with a cover story,

"Uh, yeah, my job. I got laid off. I think until they finish renovations to the building. They said something about safety and shit. I forgot," she told him.

Although a few years had gone by, George knew Conchita. He could tell when she wasn't being totally honest; but he didn't want to spoil the mood so he kept on listening.

After they ate and ordered a few more rounds they continued talking about random happenings in the world. Not wanting to stay until the doors closed, George flagged down the server, paid the tab and they quickly headed for the exit.

Once they got outside, the air was chilly and Conchita began shivering. George offered her his jacket, to which she accepted, and that's when his phone rang. Wasting no time, he took it out his coat pocket and quickly answered it,

"Hello. Hey what's up Liv," he said. While he was talking, he took a few steps away from Conchita, so as to not let her hear his full conversation. She could tell by his body language, and the fact that he kept turning his back towards her, that he was being questioned. *"Damn this mother fucker ain't loyal at all,"* she thought. After he hung up he then shuffled back towards her.

"Damn, she got you on a short leash, huh," she joked.

"No, not really. She just called to say she missed me," he said trying to conceal the fact that his relationship was far more serious than he was leading on. He was lying and Conchita knew it, but she managed to mask her anger and carry on. Then he leaned in close and whispered in her ear,

"You wanna spend the night with me?" he asked. For a minute she hesitated, but then she thought about Ri-Ri's cramped little place and quickly accepted his offer. Feeling pleased that she accepted his offer, they then walked to the nearest train station enroute to his place. Once they got to his apartment, Conchita was flabbergasted by the layout of the penthouse.

"Damn, you did well for yourself I see. Marble floors and shit," she exclaimed. He had become so use to it, he just stood there watching her admire his place. Conchita was wowed, not only by the fact that it was a swanky penthouse, because she had been in nice places before, but because it was *his* place. She knew him when he didn't have anything, so to see him go from an apartment that they shared to a penthouse apartment, she was impressed. Her feelings of admiration were short lived though and were preceded by jealousy. She was pissed off that he had shitted on her and their relationship, and then went on to flourish without her. *"This is gonna be double sweet. Ima make him leave that new bitch, then break his fuckin' heart when I leave his mother fucking ass,"* she thought. As she schemed on him, she concealed her true intentions all the while by smiling. Then she began disrobing and headed for the shower. As he stood there watching her ass jiggle, his mouth began salivating and he soon followed behind her.

When she stepped into the shower, her body was just how he remembered it. Dark black nipples, neatly shaven vagina, and jet-black hair. As her entire body became drenched, the water seemed to bounce off her nipples like liquid crystals.

"Come here," she softly said pulling him closer grabbing only his dick. Once they were chest to chest she dropped to her knees and began servicing him with her supple lips. As soon as she felt him twitch, she stopped and turned off the water. Then, she motioned for him to follow her into the living room and in front of the fire place grabbing only his throbbing member. For a second, she paused as if looking for a way to start it.

"Push that red button," he said before she could ask.

After quickly finding it, the fire place was instantly ignited and she went back to servicing him. Feeling the climax return, and not wanting to cum prematurely, he stood her up and penetrated her deeply. Once he was completely inside her, she shivered with delight. With every stroke she grew wetter and wetter, and after several thrust, she could feel him pulsating again. Not wanting the moment to end, she turned around and pushed him onto the couch.

As he sat on the sofa rock hard, she proceeded to straddle him like a wild bull. Trying to stall his orgasm he began sucking her breast and biting her nipples violently. As the sweat beaded and rolled between their bodies', the vibrations and soaked stained flesh were too much for them to handle and they immediately and simultaneously climaxed.

"Damn, did you miss me?" she asked with a euphoric expression on her face.

"Hell yeah," he said exhaustedly as he lay on the floor trying to regain his breath. Conchita then hopped up and ran to the room to retrieve her cigarettes. Moments later, she returned with a single cigarette lighting it up and then handing it to him.

"Damn that was crazy," he said inhaling the cigarette.

"I know, right," she replied.

"So now what?" he curiously asked looking at her through the smoke.

"I don't know, let's just take it slow, and see what happens," she told him. After finishing the cigarette, she laid her head on his chest and they soon drifted off to sleep. As they lay in the middle of the living room, nestled in front of the fire place, the thought hadn't even occurred to George that Liv was outraged that he hadn't spoken to her before the night was out. For this reason alone, his morning would unfold very bizarrely.

Chapter 21

Angels are evil too and demons frolic

Conchita and George slept peacefully throughout the night like angels floating on clouds in the sky. The fire place was blazing so fiercely that they didn't even need blankets. As the morning approached, the sun was peering through the blinds and the birds were chirping. The peace and serenity of this morning would be short lived though, because upon opening her eyes, Conchita realized someone standing over her with a gun. It was Liv. Startled, Conchita laid there frozen with fear.

"Hey, uh, relax," Conchita said trying to calm Liv down. Out of nowhere, Liv pistol whipped George.

"Aww," he yelled screaming in pain.

"Wake up mother-fucker," she barked. Confused and trying to keep blood from running into his eyes, he sat up.

"How the fuck did you get inside my apartment," he asked.

"I made a copy one day while you were working on your reports," she replied. "I knew it would come in handy one day. You barely spoke to me yesterday, and then you didn't even bother to call me to say goodnight. I should've known something was up," she continued.

"Liv, now calm down, don't do anything stupid," he softly said inching closer towards her. As he sweet talked her, she slowly began to lower the gun and cry. Before he could get close enough to take the gun away, Conchita pounced on her like a lion attacking an antelope. With two swift punches, Conchita incapacitated Liv; knocking her out cold. Breathing hard, Conchita then turned to George,

"Do you have any more bitches coming through the front door I should be concerned about?" she asked. George didn't even answer her; he just casually picked up his phone and called the police. While he was on the phone, Conchita headed to the bathroom to freshen up.

When she was finished, she returned to the living room to see the cops taking Liv out of the apartment in handcuffs. Then, as Conchita was heading for the door, George stopped her,

"Chi-Chi, hey come here. Don't just leave, let me explain," he pleaded. Feeling reluctant she paused and stopped,

"Look George, I'll call you later. Get your shit together," she said abrasively snatching away from him. As she walked down the hallway she began crying. What they had in college it seemed, was now gone and she felt nothing but an empty void. Walking out of the building she continued crying profusely as she headed for the nearest train station. The whole time on the train, her mind was in a daze.

As soon as she arrived at Ri-Ri's place, she pounded on the door waiting for an answer. When Ri-Ri opened the door, she sleepily looked at her.

"Yo why you knocking like the feds?" she asked. Conchita didn't respond, she just made her way to the living room and flopped across the couch. Having been awakened from her slumber, Ri-Ri was now up and alert.

"Yo what happened," she energetically asked.

"I don't wanna talk about it," Conchita replied.

"Fuck that shit; you just woke a bitch up. I was sleeping like mother fucking 'sleeping beauty' and shit, and you just gonna wake me up like that. You're gonna tell me something bitch," she said giggling. Unable to ignore Ri-Ri's prodding, she reluctantly turned around and began unloading details.

"Okay, so we went out last night and the evening was perfect. It was a perfect restaurant, a perfect conversation and all that. Then we go back to his place and it was decked out with marble floors, and a fur rug in the living room and all that shit. He made love to me in front of the fire place till we got all sweaty and shit. We ended up falling asleep right there in the living room; I mean it was beautiful. Then I wake up to a white bitch holding a gun to my face and shit," she exclaimed. "George tried to talk the bitch down, but as soon as I got an opening I hit that bitch with a two piece. I knocked her smooth the fuck out," she continued. As soon as she said that, they burst into laughter.

"Well, what you gonna' do now?" Ri-Ri asked.

"I might continue fucking with him but I don't know yet," Conchita replied.

"Must be nice, must be nice," Ri-Ri said as she got up to brew a pot of coffee.

"But look, I got a lot on my mind. Ima' take a quick nap. Wake me up in an hour," Conchita told her. Ri-Ri agreed and continued getting for ready for the day. When Conchita did wake up, several hours had past and Ri-Ri was gone. Not really having a game plan for the rest of her day, she turned on the T.V. and began watching mindless shows.

After about a half an hour or so, Ri-Ri had returned to the apartment. She quickly raced into the living room to where Conchita was.

"Yo, I met up with my guy Ahk from back in the day," she said ecstatically. "I know how we're gonna make some money till Frieda gets back in touch with us. Big money too," she continued. Curious about the news, Conchita sat up,

"Okay, I'm listening," she said.

"All we gotta do is fly to the Cayman Islands and pick up some packages. Bring them back to the states and they'll pay us $5,000 a piece," she told Conchita.

"What's in the packages?" Conchita asked.

"Who gives a fuck? I figure if we do it like six or seven times we'll be straight," Ri-Ri replied. "Look, just get that richy mother fucker to come with you. If ya'll look like a couple, no one will suspect a thing," she continued. As they sat in silence Conchita begin to think it over.

"Okay, I'm with it," Conchita told her. Elated, Ri-Ri jumped up and began celebrating.

"Yeah bitch, we bout to get this money," she exclaimed as she reached into one of her bags pulling out a bottle of champagne'. They popped open the bottle, and Ri-Ri raced into the kitchen to retrieve a couple of glasses. As soon as Ri-Ri returned, Conchita began prodding her with questions,

"So, when do we start?"

"Immediately," Ri-Ri replied.

After Conchita left, I was contacted by the 57th district precinct and asked to file a formal complaint against Liv. After taking a shower I threw on some clothes and quickly headed downtown. Once I arrived, I quickly went through the motions of speaking to a detective and filing a report. When I was finished, I made my way towards the exit, and as soon as I got outside, my cell phone rang. It was Conchita.

"Hey, you wanna go on a vacation," she asked. For a minute I paused, I hadn't been on a vacation since I started working. Now seemed like a perfect time to go.

"Sure. Where to?" I asked.

"The Cayman Islands," she replied.

"How soon are you trying to go?" I asked her.

"Tomorrow," she said.

"Uh, that soon?" I mumbled, having been caught off guard by the unexpected request. "Let me check on some things and get back to you," I told her. Elated that I was even considering going, she happily agreed and hung up.

As I walked down the street a plethora of thoughts began running through my mind. One chieftain thought in particular was, *"How did Chi-Chi have the time or money to take a vacation."* Not wanting to overthink the situation, I decided not to dwell on the idea and just go along with it. When I got back to my apartment, I quickly called the office to notify HR that I was taking a vacation. Since I had an impeccable track record, and I brought the company millions of dollars, they signed off without a thought. Then I called Conchita back to let her know that I was game. I also took the liberty of booking all the tickets so that there wasn't any delay. I was in need of some much-needed R&R. Also, to make sure we were on time for our flight, I sent a cab to pick up Conchita and her friend so we could leave from my place.

When they got to my apartment the fireplace was crackling away and the living room was nice and warm.

"Damn yo, his shit is swank. You should've asked to crash at his spot," Ri-Ri said.

"Crash at my spot?" I said confused. "Conchita what's going on," I asked.

"Nothing, Ri-Ri's just talking out her ass as usual. I'm staying at her place because I don't want Madre' to sweat me until I go back to work. If she sees me there too much she's going to start asking a bunch of questions," she replied.

"Okay, that makes sense," I said. Thinking nothing else of the matter, we spent the rest of the evening drinking wine, smoking joints and playing cards. Then, as the evening winded down, we decided to call it a night so that we could be well rested for our flight the next morning.

The night had come and gone when it was 7:30 in the morning already. When we all awakened there was no need to rush to get ready. We leisurely took turns using the bathroom. Once we were all dressed, I called a taxi cab to the airport and off we went.

Getting through security was smooth and easy, seeing as though everyone was traveling light with minimal luggage. When we finally made it off the plane, the sun seemed to beam down on us beautifully but unrelenting. The air was a fresh that I had never tasted before. In a rush to enjoy the new surroundings, Conchita and Ri-Ri quickly flagged down a taxi cab so that we could make it to the nearest hotel.

As soon as we got to the front desk, I made sure I requested a separate room so that me and Conchita could be alone most of the trip. When we got inside the room, Conchita and Ri-Ri hurriedly stripped down so that they could enjoy the pool. I decided to stay back and enjoy some wine and room service.

After a few hours of mindlessly flipping through the channels, I decided to enjoy some of the sun before it went down. When I arrived at the pool, I was surprised to find only Conchita.

"Where's ya friend Ri-Ri," I asked.

"She went to the sauna to steam out. I've been out here alone for a while now. I was wondering when you were gonna come join me," she said seductively as she swam to the edge of the pool where I was standing. "Now take off your trunks and let me do something to *your* friend," she continued. Dipping my toe into the pool, I could tell that the water was warm so I quickly obliged. As soon as I entered the pool, she completely submerged herself underwater and began sucking on me feverishly. I think she felt me twitch, as if I were about to cum, because after six strokes with her mouth she came up.

"Let's go to the sauna," she said. Quickly jumping out of the pool I agreed, and we and headed straight there. When we got to the sauna, I noticed Ri-Ri was gone.

"I thought your friend was in here," I said.

"She probably went back to her room. It *has* been a minute," she replied. "*Good*" I thought; we weren't going to be interrupted. Just to make sure Ri-Ri or anyone else didn't open the door without announcing themselves, I locked it behind us. When I turned around from securing the door I found her bent over the bench motioning for me to penetrate her.

"Put it in Papi," she said seductively with her ass in the air. Quickly darting inside her, I began stroking wildly. After climaxing, I felt like I was going to pass out from the steam. The two were a hell of combination. While lying there we decided to head back to the room for some much-needed rest.

After a few hours of sleep, I awaken in the middle of the night to find that Conchita was gone. Startled, I got up and ran out of the room hoping to find her and Ri-Ri smoking cigarettes in the hallway. When I didn't find them there my heart began pounding harder and harder with every second passing. Thinking quick on my feet, I raced back to the room and searched for my phone. I called her cell, but I got nothing but her voicemail. I called again, but still got no answer. *"What the fuck was going on?"* I thought. *"Maybe Conchita and Ri-Ri went out for a midnight swim. We were in a foreign country; where could she possibly wonder off to?"* I continued to reason. Walking back into the room, I turned on the television and poured a glass of wine. As I sat there staring at the T.V. I fell into a daze. *"Could she be up to some shit? The last time she disappeared she caught a murder charge,"* I thought. Then I reasoned, *"We are in the Cayman Islands, it's not too much she could get into here."* That sentiment gradually calmed me down and put me at ease. She'd return to the room when she got finished doing whatever it was she was doing. As I sipped my wine and watched the program on the screen, I became drowsy and drifted back to sleep.

When Conchita arrived at the local bar she spotted Ri-Ri almost immediately. Feeling a streak of nervousness run through her body, she quickly raced over to get their plan into motion.

"Damn bitch, what took you so long?" Ri-Ri asked.

"I had to wait till he was asleep and shit. Shit, *I* fell asleep, while you playing," Conchita said.

"Well you here now, that's all that matters," Ri-Ri replied. Then she took a sip of her drink and said, "Look, all we got to do is meet up with a guy named Deondre', pick up the packages and get back to the hotel room. Got it?" Absorbing the plan, Conchita nodded.

"And get a drink girl, get loose, shit!" Ri-Ri continued. After ordering a Pina colada, Conchita began scanning the dingy bar.

"How the fuck do we find this Deondre' guy?" Conchita asked.

Ri-Ri wasted no time filling her in,

"My man Ahk told me that he was about 6 feet tall and had a low hair cut with waves. I called him about ten minutes before you arrived so be on the lookout for a nigga with waves," she said.

As she watched the people mingling at the bar, Conchita spotted their mystery man from across the room.

"Yo, he's right there," she told Ri-Ri pointing towards the restrooms. Their guy must've just come out, because he was wiping his hands on his blue cashmere shirt. When Ri-Ri spotted him, she motioned for Conchita to follow her and they made their way over in his direction.

"Hola Papi," Ri-Ri said as they approached Deondre'.

"Yo, do I know you?" he asked.

"Ahk told me to holla at you when we touched down," she replied. As soon as he heard that, he smiled.

"Oh yeah, ya'll the hoes he was talking about. Okay, follow me," he said turning towards the exit door. As they followed behind him, Conchita began growing uneasy and her stomach started grumbling.

"Yo, be easy ma', ain't no one gonna hurt you. It's just business babe," he said after hearing her stomach growl. Ri-Ri tried to reassure her but Conchita was not comforted. If she decided not to go through with it, what was her game plan? Live off George and wait it out until Frieda contacted them? If Frieda did give them the go ahead, how was she going to explained to George that she was a call girl? If Frieda didn't call them back, what was she going to do then; go back to a shitty job? She couldn't live off her parent's money, her trial alone almost ate them alive. Well to do or not, they weren't rich. So hypnotically following suit, she quickly made up her mind and went along with the program. *"Six or seven times and I'm through,"* she thought. As they made their way through the pitch-black corridor, they finally made it to another entrance. Once the door opened, Conchita could see that the room was swanky and well lit. Deondre' wasted no time quickly retrieving the package from under a desk.

"Here," he said tossing it to Ri-Ri.

"That's all?" she said scanning the small package.

"The fuck you expect, fifty packages? He said laughing. "Look, make this happen and they'll be more. Hey, I'd do it myself but I ain't got anymore paid leave time," he continued. Then he gave her a little tip,

"Look I work customs at the airport. What time does your flight leave out?" he asked.

"We leave Friday at 3:30 pm," Ri-Ri replied.

"Good, I work 2pm to 10pm. When you get to your gate, text me and I'll come over there and pass you through, but you're gonna have to hide it well. Got it?" he told Ri-Ri. Without saying a word, she nodded and placed the small packages inside her purse.

"Oh, and I have to stress this last point. If you misplace, open or loose the package's *after* you leave the island, Ahk will handle the repercussions. Got it?" he told them. Once again saying nothing, Ri-Ri just nodded. Then, the mood lightened up and Deondre' offered them a drink. They quickly accepted and then began playing pool to unwind. After about four games, Conchita leaned across the pool table near Ri-Ri,

"Yo, George is probably wondering where I'm at. Let's bounce. We got what we needed; I don't want him wondering what I'm up too," she said.

"Look Mami, I'll pay for a cab for you back to the hotel. I kind of like him. Come on Chica, I wanna stay here. You got some ding a ling waiting. I want to see what's up," Ri-Ri told her. "Just tell the driver you staying at the Grand Hotel and you'll be fine," she said after handing Conchita some money. Then she kissed Conchita on the head and quickly turned her attention back to Deondre'. Conchita was reluctant at first, but seeing that Ri-Ri wasn't changing her mind, she walked out of the front door and waited for the cab to arrive. When it did, she jumped in and sped off back to the hotel.

When she got to her room, the T.V. was still on and George was passed out on the couch. Not wanting to leave him there, she woke him up and walked him back to the bed. While lying there, she quickly nestled between his arms and peacefully dozed off.

When Conchita woke up the next morning, George was still asleep. She knew he would be curious of her whereabouts the night before, so she jumped in the shower, then ordered room service to surprise him. Once the food arrived he was awakened by the aroma of the dish that she placed in front of him.

"Where'd you disappear to last night?" he calmly asked.

"Shut up and eat. I ordered the fish hash with mango chutney for you," she said evading his question. Then she continued, "I went to hang out with Ri-Ri at the Sunbeam, if you must know. It's a local club; she wanted to dance. You looked so peaceful sleeping that I didn't want to wake you Papi." Looking at her suspiciously he began devouring his food. He knew she was up to something, but just like before, he couldn't tell what. Something didn't seem right, but whatever it was, it was sure to show itself in due time.

Black Devil-Blue Eyes

Chapter 22

Let the devils play and lie

While on the Island, George and Conchita ventured off the resort, seeing the coastal front and even playing with the dolphins. The four days on the Island seemed to have breezed by, when it was already time for them to leave. Three of the four days there Ri-Ri was AWOL, but the day of their departure she made sure she was back at the hotel. An hour before the cab arrived, Ri-Ri flagged Conchita's attention,

"Chi-Chi, come in my room for a minute," she said. Forgetting about the package, Conchita quickly went to see what she wanted.

"Close the door," Ri-Ri told her once Conchita was in the room. As soon as the door was shut, Ri-Ri took out the package and began opening it. When it was opened, it contained two tangerine size rubber balls and two smaller ones.

"The big ones we're gonna have to stick up our pussy. The little ones go in your ass," Ri-Ri said. Perturbed by what she had just been told, Conchita oddly looked at Ri-Ri,

"That's not gonna fit up my pussy; and what if I have to shit?" she said. Now that they had the package, they couldn't just give it back. She would have to make a choice.

"Chica, if we don't do this they're gonna kill us. Look I'll do it first," Ri-Ri snapped. She took the big ball, squatted, and inserted it inside her pussy.

"See, it was easy," she said when she stood up. Then bending over the couch, she said, "Get the lube out of my bag. Make the ball real slippery and push it in my ass." Under pressure and low on options, Conchita raced to Ri-Ri's bag and retrieved the lube. When she returned, Ri-Ri was bent over the couch spreading her cheeks apart.

"Put it on the hole and push," she said directing Conchita. Conchita did as she was told and when the ball disappeared, Ri-Ri stood up.

"See, that was easy, it's nothing. You can do it," she told Conchita. Not having any other options, she copied exactly what Ri-Ri did with the big ball. When it was time to do the little ball, she hesitated.

"I can't do that. My ass isn't as loose as yours. Why don't you do two?" Conchita said. Growing irritated, Ri-Ri looked at her displeased and replied,

"Because if I fart it might come out of my fuckin' nose. Now stop being a little bitch. We got to catch our flight, hurry up." Bending over across the couch, Conchita reluctantly did as she was told. Ri-Ri wasn't as gentle as Conchita was with her; she just lubed the ball up and shoved it straight into Conchita's ass.

"Ow bitch, not that fast," Conchita yelled.

"How's it feel?" Ri-Ri asked her once she stood up.

"It feels like I have a turd stuck in my ass," Conchita replied wiggling her butt.

"Don't worry; you'll get used to it. It'll all be over in a few hours," Ri-Ri told her. Then they quickly continued packing the rest of their belongings and headed downstairs for their cab.

Upon arriving at the airport, Conchita felt relieved that the terminal was bustling with people.

"Maybe they'll be too busy to inspect us thoroughly," she thought.

As they begin approaching their gate, Ri-Ri texted Deondre's phone immediately. Then, while waiting in line to be searched, they spotted Deondre coming to take the other agent's place. When they were up next, they quickly put their bags onto the conveyor belt and moved forward. As Deondre patted them down, George noticed that the agent looked very familiar.

"Deondre?" he said. After frisking Ri-Ri, Deondre' stared at him for a second or so.

"Gee? Yo, it's been fuckin' forever man," he said after recognizing him. Happy to see Deondre, George tossed his bag onto the conveyor belt and gave his child hood friend a hug.

"Yo, they with you," Deondre' asked pointing at Ri-Ri and Conchita.

"Yeah, that one is my girl, well, sort of," George said pointing to Conchita. "We're just out here taking a break from life," George continued. After chatting for a few more minutes, both men traded phone numbers and shook hands. Conchita, Ri-Ri and George then continued boarding their plane.

"Damn girl that was easy," Conchita whispered to Ri-Ri.

Once they arrived back in New York City, they quickly caught a cab back to George's place. When they got inside the apartment, Conchita and Ri-Ri raced to the bathroom to expel the rubber balls from their bodies. In a rush to settle in, George paid them no mind and headed to his bedroom to decompress.

Once they were in the bathroom, Ri-Ri squatted over the tub and expelled the first ball; then the second one. The second ball took a little more force but eventually came out.

"Uh shit," she groaned when she was finished. The site of the tub was grotesque and looked like a shitty murder scene. Then she looked at Conchita,

"Your turn," she said. Conchita was visibly sickened by the whole ordeal but quickly followed suit.

"Yo are we gonna have to keep doing this shit every time?" Conchita asked once she was finished.

"Yep. Hey for the money, I'll shit out a million of these," Ri-Ri replied.

"Yo, I'm not cleaning them shit's though," she told Ri-Ri. Unphased by the mess in the tub, Ri-Ri just looked at Conchita and scowled.

"You know you're acting like a big baby, right? Yo, go see if he has some gloves or something," Ri-Ri snapped. Trying not to alert George, Conchita silently rushed off to look under the kitchen sink. Relieved that she had found some dish gloves, she snatched them and quickly raced back to the bathroom.

Once Ri-Ri finished cleaning the rubber balls, she scooped them up and placed them inside her purse.

"Yo Ima' make the drop. You stay here. I'll bring back your bread," she said hugging Conchita. Then Ri-Ri raced for the door. Feeling relieved that the whole situation was over Conchita turned on the shower and began cleaning up the mess inside the tub. This would be the first of several times they would have to go through this.

After finishing up, she then went to settle in with George for the evening. The whole night passed by with no word from Ri-Ri, and as it grew later and later, Conchita began to worry. To take her mind off of the matter she rolled up a joint.

"Are you okay Chi-Chi? George asked. "You haven't really said much since we got back," he continued. Still in deep thought, she twirled the joint in his direction.

"I'm cool. You wanna puff," she replied. Taking her word for face value, he reached for the joint and took in a deep pull. After they finished smoking, they made love and peacefully drifted off to sleep.

The next day, Conchita was awakened by her phone ringing off the hook.

"Hello," she sleepily answered. It was Ri-Ri on the other end.

"Yo wake yo sleepy ass up bitch," Ri-Ri said giggling. "I'm on 145th and Lennox, come meet me at the McDonalds," she continued. While listening to Ri-Ri ramble over the phone, Conchita stared at George. He was knocked out. Not wanting to wake him, she slid out of the bed like a snake in the bushes.

"Okay girl, I'm leaving now. I'll see you there," she said before hanging up.

The train ride there didn't take long and when she arrived at the McDonalds, Ri-Ri was outside puffing a cigarette.

"Damn that was fast," Ri-Ri said.

"Yo, where's the money?" Conchita asked impatiently.

"Right here," Ri-Ri said opening a McDonald's bag. "Yo I couldn't count it earlier because I was too scared. Plus, there were too many people around. Let's go to my crib and count it," she continued. They agreed and then quickly headed for the nearest station.

Once they got to Ri-Ri's apartment they quickly proceeded to count all of the money. It was exactly $5,000.

"Damn girl, all this for those little balls?" Conchita said. Ri-Ri smiled and nodded.

"Yep and there's more," Ri-Ri replied.

After a few hours had gone by, Ri-Ri's phone rang. It was Ahk. He was so pleased with how smooth the trip went that he told her that he had five more runs lined up for them. While talking to Ahk, she quickly scrounged for a pen and pad to write down the days they needed to leave. After hanging up she turned to Conchita,

"Yo, we gotta leave in two days," she said. This routine of going back and forth continued for the next two weeks.

By week three, Conchita was so busy that George was becoming more and more curious. To ease his concerns, she decided to bring him along so he could relax and they could spend some time together. She didn't want him getting any more curious then he already was. Kicking into high gear, she booked a flight for Friday morning and when the day came they were off.

This time she left without Ri-Ri. It wasn't a run trip so she figured she didn't need the unnecessary company. After two days of prowling the city, she persuaded George to buy a little beachfront house so they could have a place to crash instead of spending money at a hotel. It wasn't big or extravagant, but it was comfy and cheap. At first, he was hesitant but the more talking she did, eventually he gave in. Excited, she texted Ri-Ri the news of the beachfront purchase.

Later that night, they celebrated with wine, a fine meal, and lots of nasty sex. In the middle of the night, after they had passed out, her phone began vibrating. She turned off the ringer earlier so that she could cut out any distractions and focus solely on George. At first, she tried to ignore it, but it wouldn't stop.

"Who the fuck is this," she muttered. She looked at the caller I.D. and quickly realized it was Ri-Ri. Not wanting to disturb George while he slept, she silently slipped out of bed and into the living room.

"What girl," she whispered. Hearing the irritation in Conchita's voice, Ri-Ri got straight to the chase,

"Yo, I know you're with your boo, but Deondre wanted to know if you could pick something up," Ri-Ri said.

"Right now?" Conchita replied.

"No girl, tomorrow," Ri-Ri told her. "Look, ya'll leave Sunday night, right? So just make up an excuse to get out of his sight. Tell him you're going to get some wine for later, I don't know, just make something up. Since you got a spot, we can bring it back here next time me and you go down there," Ri-Ri continued. Conchita had no intentions of making this a business trip, but the idea of more money made her cave.

"Okay girl. Now stop calling me, I'm trying to enjoy myself," she told Ri-Ri.

"Alright, you're right, my bad. I'll see you later," Ri-Ri replied before hanging up. Afterwards, Conchita quietly retuned to bed with George.

In the morning, before George woke up, she threw on her clothes and quickly left the house. Wasting no time, she raced to the club where they had previously met Deondre. When she arrived, he was already there standing outside. *"He must've been waiting,"* she thought as she opened the car door.

"Damn, Ri-Ri said you'd be coming by in the morning but I didn't know it would be *this* early," he said.

"I'm trying to chill with my man and this is fucking it up," she replied rolling her eyes.

"Wait, George doesn't know?" he asked with a puzzled look on his face.

"No, and I'd like to keep it that way if you don't mind," she said snatching the bag out of his hands.

"Hey, me and George go way back but I don't wanna spoil business. My mouth is zipped," he said scanning her with his eyes. "Ya'll have fun now," he continued with a big shit eating grin on his face. Paying him no mind, she hopped into the rental and quickly pulled off.

When she returned, George was still asleep. Not wanting to be caught with the package, she ran downstairs to the basement and placed the bag behind the water heater. Then she rushed back upstairs, stripped naked and slipped back into bed. He was so sound asleep that he hadn't even noticed her creep off. The rest of the trip was peaceful.

Almost as soon as she returned to the states, she was leaving out of town again with Ri-Ri. When their plane landed, they were met by Deondre' at the east terminal. He didn't even get out of the Benz to greet them. They didn't give a fuck though; they just opened the doors and jumped in. As soon as they sat down, Deondre wasted no time questioning Conchita.

"Hey Conchita, did you take that package with you when you left"? he asked.

"No, I left it here. George doesn't know what I'm doing, you know that, and I didn't want to chance him finding out either. I figured we'd pick it up when me and Ri-Ri came back," she said looking at him in the rear-view mirror.

"Okay. Just make sure ya'll move it. I got some more shit for ya'll. I don't want ya'll to get backed up," he said studying her through the mirror. Irritated at what sounded like a demand Conchita snapped,

"Yo, we didn't even ask for that shit. You wanted *me* to pick it up. We'll move it when we fuckin' get around to it. Are you sticking balloons up your ass?" she replied.

"Okay, be cool Mami, I was just asking," he told her. Then turning his attention to Ri-Ri he continued, "Yo ya girl is feisty."

"Yeah, she hasn't gotten use to filling her ass yet. Shit still grosses her out," Ri-Ri said giggling. As Deondre' and Ri-Ri made fun of her, the trio continued down the road driving straight to Conchita's beachfront.

After they got to the house, Deondre' spent an hour filling balloons with heroin.

"Hey, why don't we all chill tonight? Smoke some good' before you ladies' jet out tomorrow. I'll be free after eight," Deondre' said after he was finished portioning the rubber balls. Ri-Ri was down; she liked kicking it with Deondre'. He was her relief whenever she was there. Conchita on the other hand, just liked coming into town, picking up packages and preparing for the next day's flight out. She also didn't trust Deondre'. Whenever he was around she was always catching him stare at her with a creepy look on his face, but she didn't want to be a downer and spoil Ri-Ri's visit, so she agreed to it just to get along. Pleased that they had taken him up on his request he smiled and headed for the door.

While waiting until Deondre' returned, they sat in the living room sipping glasses of Sangria and smoking joints. As the time neared closer to eight o'clock, Ri-Ri jumped into the shower to freshen up. Conchita didn't even bother. While lying there, she began thinking about George. She never did call him when she was out of town. Being that he didn't know what she was up to, she didn't like feeling guilty. As her mind continued racing back at fourth, suddenly her phone rang. After grabbing it and checking the caller I.D. she realized it was him. "*What the fuck. He must have telepathy*," she thought to herself. At first, she wasn't going to answer it, but she knew that he'd keep calling so she reluctantly did.

"Hey Papi," she softly said.

"Hey baby, what's up? I hadn't heard from you. I thought I'd give you a ring just to hear your voice," he told her. When she heard that her heart began to melt.

"Oh, that's so sweet," she replied.

"Hey, I was wondering if you'd like to get together tonight," he asked. As soon as he said that, a streak of fear jilted throughout her entire body. What was she going tell him? That she was in the Cayman Island smuggling dope? She had to think fast.

"I can't Papi, me and Ri-Ri gotta work late tonight. Let's do it tomorrow," she said. After he heard that there was a brief silence over the phone,

"What do you do again?" he asked.

"I work at that Ihop in East Brooklyn. I forgot to tell you. Ri-Ri's aunt got us on over there. I've been tired a lot and it must've skipped my mind," she said thinking even quicker on her toes. He must've not believed her, because there was a long silence over the phone before he replied.

"Yeah, alright," he said sounding disappointed. His response was so low, that Conchita barely heard him.

"Hello, baby you there?" she nervously asked.

"Yeah I'm here. Okay, tomorrow I guess it is. I got a lot of work to catch up on anyways so I guess that's cool," he told her. The sound of his voice made her feel guilty all over again. It was like round two of their previous relationship.

"I'll see you tomorrow Papi. I promise," she said softly.

After hanging up, she laid there staring at the ceiling when suddenly, Deondre' arrived. When he walked into the living room, a strong odor of marijuana followed him. Conchita's demeanor quickly lightened up upon noticing the variety of liquor he brought with him. Trying not to dwell on George, she darted into the kitchen to retrieve some glasses. When she returned, Ri-Ri was exiting the backroom wearing nothing but a thong. Excited to see Deondre', Ri-Ri ran over to give him a hug. After smearing him with kisses she raced over to the stereo and selected some smooth, relaxing music. Then, spotting the weed on the table, Ri-Ri quickly hopped on the sofa and began rolling up a fat joint. They then filled their glasses up with champagne and toasted to their success.

Later that evening, Deondre' took off his pistol and set it on the table so he could relax comfortably. The sight of the gun didn't unnerve either one of them, as they had grown accustom to seeing guns in their line of work. The weed was so high-powered Ri-Ri kept fading in and out of consciousness. As the music continued playing in the background, Deondre' kissed Ri-Ri's legs; but she was too high to engage him, and all his attempts seemed to go unnoticed. Realizing this, he shifted his attention to Conchita, darting his eyes between her legs and breast. Growing tired of him staring at her, she decided to call it a night. Placing her glass on the table, she quickly got up and headed for the master bedroom. Feeling as though she drank too much, she stopped in the bathroom to relieve her bladder, but before she could finish washing her hands, Deondre' crept inside.

"What the fuck are you doing in here? She yelled.

"Shoo', you're gonna wake Ri-Ri up," he quietly said walking towards her. When he got up on her, she felt fear run through her entire body. Before she could scream he placed one hand over her mouth and the other over her throat.

"If you keep trying to scream, I'm gonna' choke you till you can't breathe," he coldly told her. Then he tightened his grip around her neck while fumbling to loosen his pants. Conchita began freaking out. She wanted to scream, but the grip he had around her neck was blocking her windpipe. She tried hitting him, but her one hundred and thirty-five pounds was no match for his large frame. Figuring there was nothing else she could do, she gave up and let him violently penetrate her. As he began pumping inside her, his grip seemed to have weakened and that's when she made her move. She was too tired from struggling to punch him anymore, so the only thing she could think to do was to bite his neck. As soon as she bit him, it sent him into a fit of rage. He began choking her even harder and more violently than before. "*I'm gonna die,*" she thought. She was terrified, and worst of all, there was nothing she could do about it.

Then, just as her eyes began to close, she saw Ri-Ri enter the bathroom. Deondre was so distracted that he was totally oblivious of Ri-Ri. Even worse, the gun she had pointed directly at his head. When he heard the hammer cock back, he stopped instantly and stood motionless.

"You piece of shit. Get off of her," Ri-Ri said. "Mami, come over here," she continued. Overjoyed that Ri-Ri had intervened, she quickly adjusted her clothes and ran behind her. "What you wanna do," she asked Conchita. Wasting no time, Conchita took the gun and fired point blank into Deondre's head. Blood splattered all over the bathroom mirror and his slumped body hit the floor with a thud.

Before Conchita could savor the moment though, Ri-Ri started going berserk,

"I-didn't-mean-kill-him," Ri-Ri said with a bewildered look on her face. "You know, like shoot his balls, foot, leg. I don't know, anything but don't kill him!" she continued.

"The mother fucker was raping me. What the fuck was I supposed to do? And on top of all that, he was trying to kill me!" Conchita yelled. Then with the gun still clinched tight in her fist, she turned to Ri-Ri and continued, "Yo grab ya shit, we gotta go, now!"

While scrambling for their belongings, throwing whatever clothes in their duffle bag, Ri-Ri grabbed Conchita's arm and asked,

"What about the dope?"

"Get what you think you can stuff. We'll boof em' in the airport bathroom. Whatever we leave behind will only have *his* prints on em," Conchita replied. Sounding like a good plan, they ran back into the living room, retrieved some of the dope, then bolted out of the front door. While waiting for the cab, Ri-Ri looked at Conchita,

"Yo what about this?" she said holding the gun. Trying not to panic, Conchita quickly snatched it out of Ri-Ri's hands and wiped it down. Then, while pacing in a circle, an idea struck her.

"I got it," she said before running behind the house. When she returned Ri-Ri looked at her confused,

"What you do with it?" Ri-Ri asked with a perplex look on her face.

"I threw it into the sea. The tide will carry it away. They'll never find that shit," Conchita said smiling. Ri-Ri smiled back at her, and as soon as they began victory dancing, their cab drove up.

When they got to the airport, they quickly followed the plan and ran to the bathroom. After purchasing their tickets, they nervously waited in line to board their plane. So as not to draw attention to themselves, they didn't stand in line together. When Conchita was next, she was patted down and let through the boarding gate with no problem. When it was Ri-Ri's turn, at the exact moment, an agent walked pass her with a k-9 dog. The dog quickly ran up to Ri-Ri and started barking. Conchita couldn't make out what the customs agents were saying to Ri-Ri, but they quietly escorted her out of line. *"I hope she doesn't mention me,"* she thought to herself. Not wanting to draw any attention, Conchita quickly boarded the plane and waited for takeoff. The flight seemed to last forever, and her anxiety of flying, coupled with Ri-Ri's arrest at the airport, had her on pins and needles. Feeling like she was under surveillance, when the plane landed she quickly exited the building.

Once she was outside, she called up a cab and chained smoke until it arrived. When it did, she gave the driver directions straight to George's house. It was still early in the day, so he wouldn't be home until after six. That didn't bother her though, she figured she'd just wait at the local coffee shop until later on in the evening.

While sipping her latte', her mind was racing a mile a minute. The trauma of being assaulted, shooting Deondre' and Ri-Ri's arrest all raced around in her head at once. What if Ri-Ri rolled on her? What would she do? She couldn't go back to prison. What if Deondre's people found a way to retaliate? How would she ward them off? Lastly, what if she contracted a disease from Deondre'? While the thoughts were racing around in her head, she had totally forgot about the drugs in the basement. This would prove to be her ultimate undoing.

When six o'clock finally came around, she hurriedly got up and began making her way to George's place. As soon as she got near his apartment building, she could see him approaching about a block down the street. So as not to cause alarm, she decided to wait at the front entrance until he walked up. When he approached the front door, he instantly spotted her.

"Hey Mami, are you okay? You look like you had a rough night," he said. Happy to see him, she rushed to give him a hug. His warm embrace seemed to put her at ease. Up until now, she had planned to pay him back for cheating on her and for not coming to see her while she was locked up, but those things didn't seem to matter to her anymore. Instantly she knew that he would always be there for her.

"Baby, I'm so sorry," she said as she began to cry.

"Sorry for what, for last night? Yo' don't worry about it. It's all good," he said cluelessly. She knew he didn't know what she meant, but it didn't matter. All that mattered was that he was there for her and she finally felt safe.

Black Devil-Blue Eyes

188

Chapter 23
The devil's repentance

Over the next few weeks' things seemed to be going very well for Conchita. She had gotten tested and the results were negative for everything. It turns out, that dirty bastard Deondre' didn't have anything. She was relieved for that. None of Ahk's people knew about her, so retaliation wasn't even a factor anymore. She was very relieved by that. She and George were spending more time together and things seemed to getting back to normal. Frieda had even called her back for more work. Turns out, those clients had a little dirt on them also, and didn't feel the need to pursue the matter further. She hadn't heard at all from Ri-Ri, but Conchita figured she would manage to finagle her way out of that situation. She was wrong.

One day while lounging around, she got a call. It was Ri-Ri.

"Bitch, what the fuck is up," Ri-Ri angrily asked as soon as Conchita answered.

"Girl what happened?" Conchita replied.

"They found the stuff on me. They're charging me with trafficking and shit. My public defender say's the least I'll get is five years," Ri-Ri told her.

"Well why you sound pissed at me?" Conchita asked.

"Because it's been three weeks and you ain't even checked on me or bailed me out!" she barked.

"Yo I'm so sorry. My mind was fucked up, especially after what happened. I got scared for a minute and George has been the only thing that has gotten me through all this. I still haven't told him anything though," Conchita said.

"Shit you don't have to. Since I've been in here they've questioned me about Deondre' *and* George. It seems that Deondre' listed ya man as his next of kin after they ran back into each other," Ri-Ri replied. "They done connected George's beachfront to Deondre' and I think they gonna wanna talk to him soon," Ri-Ri continued. After hearing that, Conchita's heart sank into her stomach. Not because of the murder, she had thrown the gun into the sea. There's no way they would be able to link that to *anyone*, but at that moment she remembered that she had stashed the previous package of dope in the basement behind the water heater. Figuring there wasn't anything she could do about it, she decided not to dwell on the idea and see how things played out.

"How much is your bail?" she asked Ri-Ri focusing on the issue at hand.

"$5,000, and there's no 10% either. They want the whole amount," Ri-Ri told her.

"I'll be there tomorrow," she said, feeling relieved Ri-Ri hadn't said anything to the authorities.

When George got home, she explained to him that she had to go to work the next evening and that she would probably crash at Ri-Ri's spot, so as not to cause him concern. He gladly accepted the news and they continued with the rest of the evening enjoying each other's company.

The next day, before the sun came up, Conchita jumped out of bed and into action. As she threw on her clothes she looked at George still peacefully sleeping. After she got dressed she kissed him on the cheek, quickly left the apartment, and headed for the airport.

The flight seemed to last only a couple of hours until she arrived on the island, but once she was off the plane she quickly flagged down a cab and directed him to the local jail. When she arrived at the precinct she went through the motions of posting Ri-Ri's bail then waited patiently in the lobby. After sitting in the cold room for a couple of hours, Ri-Ri finally appeared. Her face lit up as soon as she spotted Conchita sitting in the lobby.

"Chica, you came," she said hugging Conchita.

"Of course, I did. What you thought, I was gonna' leave you here to rot in this bitch?" Conchita told her.

"I don't know Mami. I *have* been in here for a minute," Ri-Ri said rolling her eyes. Conchita paid the comment no mind and hugged her again. After their quick embrace though, Conchita's mood shifted drastically.

"We gotta go by the house. I gotta find that shit. If the police find it, George is gonna be fucked up," she told Ri-Ri. Puzzled, Ri-Ri just looked at her,

"What, why? I thought you was gonna pay him back when you got out of jail anyways. Well here it is," Ri-Ri said.

"I *was*, but then I got to thinking; *I* put me in jail. Not him. *I* stashed that stuff at his place. Not him. It's not right that he gotta pay for some shit that I did," Conchita explained. As she listened to her reasoning Ri-Ri shook her head.

"Well let's hurry up before our flight tonight," Ri-Ri told her. They called up a cab and took off heading to the beachfront.

When they arrived, there was caution tape around the entire house. To make sure no one was around, Conchita asked the driver to wait while she got out and checked. Once she made a full search of the entire perimeter, she walked to the back door and began to pry open a window. It took her several attempts to crack open, but once she did, she was able to casually slip inside. Not knowing how long she had, she immediately raced towards the basement to retrieve the package. When she reached behind the water heater and didn't feel it, she was jolted with fear.

"Fuck!" she shouted. Trying not to panic, she quickly began searching the entire basement. "*Maybe I moved it around and forgot,*" she thought. After not finding it, she gave up and ran back upstairs. Once she was outside, she quickly darted back to the cab.

"Was it still there?" Ri-Ri asked.

"Hell no, girl, they must've found it," Conchita replied.

"Okay so now what?" Ri-Ri asked puzzled.

"I guess I'll just have to wait and see what happens," Conchita told her.

"Has Frieda called you back yet?" Ri-Ri asked.

"Yeah, she's called me, but she's still mad at you," Conchita said calmly.

"Girl, fuck that bitch. She better not be trippin'. She's the reason that shit went down the way it did," Ri-Ri quipped.

"Stop being a baby and chill the fuck out. No one told you to bring a gun that night. Ms. Gold pussy! Who you thought you was, a James Bond villain?" Conchita said making fun of Ri-Ri. As the cab sped away they continued laughing and joking about Frieda.

When they reached the airport they immediately raced to the ticket booth to purchase Ri-Ri's ticket. Afterwards, they went to a quiet little bar to kill some time. When it was time for them to board their flight they quickly got in line, and as with before, they made sure not to stand next to each other.

While standing in line, out of the corner of her eye, Conchita spotted a customs agent walking with a k-9 dog. As soon as she seen that, she began sweating uncontrollably.

"Oh fuck," she mumbled trying to remain calm. To take her mind off the dog, she focused straight ahead and went through the motions of being search. When it was her turn, she went through without a hitch. Glad that she had made it through, Conchita quickly raced toward the ramp entrance. Knowing that Ri-Ri was clean this time, she didn't even look back as she entered the plane.

Once inside, they quickly found their seats and sat down. As soon as the plane took off and the captain went through his monologue they waited for the flight attendant to begin her beverage routine. After they thoroughly got drunk they quickly fell asleep and let the plane take them safely home. If it wasn't for the abrupt wakeup call they probably would've slept forever. As the plane begin to empty, the flight attendant approached them,

"Excuse me ladies but the plane has landed," she softly said. Startled, Conchita and Ri-Ri quickly began retrieving their bags from the overhead compartment. When they made it out of the airport, they quickly flagged down a cab. Once they hopped inside, Ri-Ri gave the driver a $50 bill and directed him to her apartment.

When they arrived, Ri-Ri raced upstairs and inside the unit.

"Ugh, I'm so glad to be home. They barely let me take a shower while I was there. My pussy is *so* crusty girl," Ri-Ri said as she shed her clothes. While Ri-Ri went to freshen up, Conchita settled into the living and flopped across the couch. To take her mind off the missing package, she stared at the ceiling day dreaming about the last time she made love to George. As she zoned out, her thoughts were quickly interrupted by her phone ringing. It was George.

"Hey Mami, where'd you go to? I know you were going to spend the night at Ri-Ri's, but I thought I'd see you before you left," he said.

"I'm sorry, I had to do some running around baby," she replied.

"It's all good," he told her. "Well, when you get off work, call me so I know that you made it in safe. We can link up tomorrow when I get off work," he continued.

"Okay baby, I'll do that," she said before hanging up. Then as she sat back, she felt her anxiety returning. Just when it felt like her heart was going to bust out of her chest, Ri-Ri peered from around the corner.

"Yo, is everything cool with ya man?" Ri-Ri asked. Totally ignoring Ri-Ri's question, Conchita hopped up off the couch and ran into the bathroom to throw up. Not finding that package was causing her to have a panic attack.

Later that night, Ri-Ri took the rubber balls that Conchita had managed to smuggle from before, and said that she was going to see Ahk.

Yo, you got ya' pistol?" Conchita asked while Ri-Ri searched for her jacket. Caught off guard by the question, Ri-Ri paused for a second before answering.

"Ain't nothing gonna happen. Me and Ahk go way back. He ain't gonna think we had nothing to do with Deondre's murder. And as for as that package, I'll just explain to him that the police must've found it. Relax Chica. I'll be fine," Ri-Ri told her. Then she grabbed her purse and hugged Conchita before quickly exiting the unit.

After Ri-Ri left, Conchita stood at the door as her heart sank into her stomach. She hoped her friend would return, but she had a bad feeling about the whole situation. **Little did she know, that would be the last time she'd ever see Ri-Ri again.** Trying to shake the eerie feeling, Conchita quickly went and flopped back across the couch. As her mind raced a mile a minute, she soon became tired and drifted off to sleep.

About two hours later, her slumber was cut short when she was awakened by a loud knock at the door.

"Who the fuck is banging on the door like the fuckin' police," she grumbled. When she opened the door, she was surprised to see it *was* the police.

"Good evening ma'am. I'm Detective Wentzler. Are you kin to a Ms. Rhiandalia Diaz?" the dumpy white man asked. As soon as he asked that, a gut-wrenching feeling shot through her stomach.

"Yeah, I'm her sister," she said lying to the detective.

"Can we come inside," he asked. She agreed and quickly led them into the living room. Before the detective told her the news, she already knew.

"Tonight Ms. Diaz was found shot to death on a hundred and forty fifth behind a McDonalds," he told her. "Do you know if she had any enemies?" he continued. Not wanting to disclose the series of events that had previously occurred, she lied again.

"No, I don't know of anyone that would want to kill my sister," she told the detective. "Anyways, how did you guys even know that she lived here? This is her mother's apartment," she asked. Puzzled by the question, the detective paused at the inquiry before answering.

"We found her I.D. card in her back-pocket ma'am. That was the only thing she had on her person. No wallet, no purse; no nothing.

Although her I.D. didn't list her current address, we traced her mother's whereabouts and she led us here," he flatly explained.

"*That was odd*," she thought. She distinctly remembered Ri-Ri taking her purse with her before she left. Upon hearing that, it was confirmation that Ahk *had* killed her. But she had never met him, and didn't know anything about him, to direct the police *to* him. After further questioning the detectives gave up. They told Conchita where she could view the body and gave her their cards in case she had further information. She told them she would and then escorted them back outside.

After closing the door, she began sobbing uncontrollably. "*Why didn't Ri-Ri take her gun with her? Why didn't I smuggle that last package when I had the chance?*" she thought. Feeling like the walls were closing in, she got up began packing a duffle bag full of clothes. She didn't know if Ri-Ri had given her up to Ahk, but she wasn't going to stick around to find out. Before leaving, she made sure she grabbed Ri-Ri's gun from inside her lower sock drawer. If Ri-Ri *did* tell him anything she wasn't gonna get caught slipping, she'd be ready. As far as she was concerned, Deondre' got what he deserved.

When she got to George's place, she knocked on the door but it seemed as if he wasn't home. Then, as she was turning to leave the door opened.

"Hey Chi-Chi!" he said. When she heard his voice, she quickly turned around and raced to give him a hug.

"I'm glad to see you too, but I thought you were coming by in the morning," he said with a puzzled look on his face.

"I was, but I couldn't wait so I called off tonight. I needed you to hold me," she told him.

"Okay baby, I will. Is everything alright?" he replied.

"Now it is," she said kissing him on the cheek. Now that she was in his arms she felt safe again. Anything could be happening to her, but when she felt his gentle touch, she felt secure. Wanting to enjoy the rest of the evening, he wasted no time quickly pulling her into the penthouse and shutting the door.

Black Devil-Blue Eyes

Chapter 24
Hell, and Heaven collide

When Conchita awakened the next morning, she eagerly got up and began cooking breakfast for George. After he had eaten and was finishing getting dressed, he quickly bolted from the apartment for work. The day was starting off beautifully for the two, but that was going to be short lived by the middle of the day.

Soon after, Conchita decided to jump into the shower and lounge around. When she was done, her intentions were to lay back and watch some television. Those plans were soon dashed, because as soon as she had gotten comfortable her phone starting ringing.

"Hello," she answered. It was Frieda on the other end.

"Bitch, you awake?" Frieda barked. With all the shit that had happened in the last few weeks Conchita figured she's slow down on dates, but as soon as Frieda started talking numbers, she quickly reconsidered. After gathering all the information from Frieda, she hung up and began dressing for a mid-day date.

At work I couldn't help but think about Conchita. While I tried to concentrate, thoughts of her sexy smile kept distracting me. When noon arrived I quickly left with a coworker to get some lunch. Maybe if I got some food in my system I could refocus my attention. While enjoying my spring rolls and listening to my coworker jabber about nothing, I couldn't help but notice a woman that eerily resembled Conchita. She was sitting at a booth across from a very tall, heavy set gentleman. "*What the fuck is she doing?*" I thought. "*Maybe it wasn't her. Maybe my mind was playing tricks on me,*" I continued to reason.

But staring harder, it became apparent that it *was* her. At first, I considered walking over to her, but then something told me to wait. I had all the time in the world and she *was* staying at my house.

Once I got home, I would question her then. If she lied to me, I'd just throw her out. Weighing my options, I went with the latter and continued eating while listening to my co-worker rambling on about nonsensical things.

When I returned to my office, I began growing angry over what I had witnessed earlier. "*How could she be seeing someone else?*" I thought. Trying to make sense of it all, I quickly began analyzing the situation critically, "*okay I see what this is, she's probably paying me back from when we were in college,*" I told myself. The notion that she was probably being spiteful for my past transgressions made it easier to accept. As soon as I began refocusing my attention on my work though, two men dressed in black slacks and blue jackets were walking towards my office door.

"Hi Mr. Sphinx, we'd like a word with you for a minute," the first man said. The seriousness of his tone puzzled me at first, and put me on high alert. As soon as I welcomed them into my office the second gentleman closed the door. When they took a seat, the first man wasted no time questioning me.

"Mr. Sphinx, we're with the F.B.I. and we have a few questions we'd like ask you," he said. "We've discovered the body of a man by the name of Deondre Rivera deceased inside a beachfront property you recently purchased. We also noticed that he listed you as his next of kin in his employment records. We're figuring he did that, because we checked, and all of his relatives are deceased.

Do you know why someone would want Mr. Rivera dead?" he continued. I was completely in shock. Conchita and I had only been to the beachfront maybe twice.

"I don't know anything about that; I've only been there a couple of times since I bought it. I know Deondre' from way back, but he's never been at my house while I was there. Maybe someone broke in, that must've happened while I was here," I replied. Halfway believing my story he looked at me pensively.

"Yeah, we figured you had nothing to do with the murder, because we checked, and you were at work. There wasn't any sign of forced entry though, which leads us to believe someone you know *was* there," he said. Instantly Conchita popped into my mind. I had given her a key, and she had been acting very secretive the last few weeks. Pissed off for what I had witnessed earlier, I still wasn't going to mention anything about her to the Fed's. I loved her. Whatever had taken place, she was going to confess to me and we'd try to figure out the rest of the details later. So, I continued to lie.

"I don't know of anyone that could've done that. I was here. Maybe ya'll should check with the authorities there to see if anyone seen anything because I got nothing," I told them. As if the agent was looking straight through me he continued,

"Yeah, okay Mr. Sphinx. We're going to continue investigating, but if we come up with nothing, you may be charged with facilitating and operating a drug house. Considering that Deondre's body was found with drugs around it, and there was a package in the basement containing heroin. Worst case scenario, you could be charged with accessory to homicide," he said.

"Homicide? I didn't kill anyone though," I told him. While detailing Deondre's murder, the detective began showing me pictures of his deceased body. Studying the pictures, I noticed that Deondre' had a bite mark on his neck. The same devil shaped mark that Conchita used to leave on me when we were in college. Things were now getting bizarre. As I tried to make sense of the information at hand, I refocused my attention back on the detective.

"Best case scenario, you'd be charged only with facilitating a drug house like I said before. So, if you know more then what you're telling us, it's in your best interest to say something now," he told me. Staying true to my initial story, I held my ground,

"Like I said before, I don't know who could've done what you're claiming. I was here working. I know just as much as you guy's.... nothing," I said. Before leaving, they stared me down then exited my office. At this point, I was perplexed *and* confused. "*What the fuck had Conchita gotten into? And why the hell was Deondre' at my beachfront? Were they fucking?*" I thought. Tonight, Conchita would have a lot of explaining to do. After that, I couldn't even get back to work. I was having such a hard time concentrating, that I decided to take the rest of the day off. Wasting no time, I shut my computer off, grabbed my blazer, and quickly exited the office. As I was leaving the building, I thought of calling Conchita but quickly dismissed the idea. Whatever I had to say, it was gonna wait. I wanted to see her face. I could tell when she was lying. Seeing her facial expressions would tell me everything I needed to know.

When I got home, I tossed my things onto the floor and flopped across the couch. I was still stunned from the information I received earlier. Not to mention, seeing Conchita with another man was bugging the hell out of me. "*Why was Chi-Chi so got damn sneaky?*" I thought. As I was brooding over the whole situation, suddenly Conchita walked through the door. As soon as she saw me, she smiled.

"Hey, Papi. You're home early," she said. Upon hearing her eager voice, I sat up and adjusted my tie.

"Chi-Chi, have a seat," I told her. She complied and quickly sat down.

"Baby, what's the matter," she asked. Feeling disappointed, I took a deep breath,

"What the fuck have you been up too Chi-Chi? Cause I had two F.B.I. agents at my fuckin' job today, questioning me about a murder at our mother-fucking beachfront!" I yelled. By the look her face I could tell she was about to drop a bomb on me.

"Baby I've been smuggling drugs back into the country for the past month. You know that guy Deondre? He was our contact to get the packages. Then he'd make sure we made it through customs without being caught. After you guys ran back into each other, Ri-Ri and I went back several times afterwards," she said.

"Why? I thought you had a job at Ihop! Why would you do that shit?" I yelled.

"I don't work at Ihop baby. I lied. I'm an escort," she said.

"An escort?" I said while adjusting my collar.

"Yes baby, an escort. I hated working at that fuckin café' so I started escorting, but then I had to find another way to make some money after Ri-Ri shot one of our clients. Our handler told us we'd have to wait until things died down. While we were waiting, Ri-Ri said she knew a guy that wanted us to bring some stuff over, so I went along with it. I was only gonna do it a few times and then stop," she replied.

"Well who the fuck killed Deondre'? I don't give a fuck about the drugs, Deondre was my friend!" I yelled.

"I did. I killed Deondre. I didn't know he was a close friend, baby! I'm so sorry," she replied.

"Well why the fuck did they find his dead body in *my* house!" I asked still perplexed. When I asked her that, she paused for a brief second before replying.

"On my last trip there, he tried to rape me baby," she softly said. As soon as she told me that I felt like a ton of bricks had just fallen on me. I sat back on the couch and tried absorbing what I had just heard. I was stunned. Here I was thinking we were getting reacquainted and she wasn't even the same woman. I was disgusted by the whole situation.

"Give me my keys and get the fuck out," I said. I didn't know what else to tell her. She was selling her body, smuggling drugs and now she was tied to a murder, *again*. I don't know what made me angrier; that fact that she had killed my childhood friend; was smuggling drugs; was escorting or the fact that she had dragged me into all her bullshit.

"Papi, I didn't mean for any of this to happen, I just didn't know how to tell you," she pleaded. I was so pissed off that I wasn't trying to hear any of it. I just wanted the lies and confusion to be over with. Seeing that I wasn't changing my mind, she just hung her head low and began crying. I didn't even sit long enough to let her tears bother me. While she sat there sobbing, I got up and began pouring a drink. After taking a sip I looked at her,

"Are you done?" I coldly asked. She didn't even bother looking up at me; she just continued crying.

"If it's any consolation, I'm not gonna mention any of this to the Feds. They can't tie the murder to me; and I think I can fight the drug charge that they're planning to pin on me. So, I guess you're off the hook. I just want you away from me. You're too much trouble and I can't trust you. You're not the same Conchita I fell in love with," I told her. With tears in her eyes she looked at me and pleaded,

"But I am papi, I swear I am." She pleaded with me but I wasn't trying to hear it. She had drastically altered my perception of her and it would never be the same. Realizing that I wasn't budging on my decision, she slowly got up and began retrieving her belongings. After she was done, she walked towards the door then looked at me.

"I love you Papi," she said. I was so pissed off that I didn't even look at her. I just kept sipping my drink.

"Just make sure you close my door," I coldly told her. As angry as I was though, I was most incensed at the web of lies she had spun. After all that, how was I just supposed to go back to normal with her? Never mind the fact that the Feds were on my ass for something I didn't do. As I sat back down on the couch, I continue to be consumed by heartbreak.

The next several months would be the most tumultuous time of my life. First, it started with being indicted for operating and facilitating a drug house and accessory to murder. I lost my job when the news broke of my indictment to my employers. While going to trial, I was forced to sale my beachfront home to cover my legal expenses. All in all, it ended with the murder charge being dismissed due to lack of evidence. The drug charge's stuck though, and I was sentenced to 10 years in a federal prison with the possibility of parole after 4 years. The only reason they continued to pursue that charge, was because the prosecutor felt like I was protecting someone. They were right. I was. So now, I'm inmate #22036G and life for me is drastically different. No more leisure trips whenever I want. No swanky penthouse with marble floors and granite countertops. No quarterly bonuses that I can stock pile and collect interest on, just three hot's and a cot. I now feel like when I seen her in that café, I should've just kept walking. The only reason I didn't roll over on her was because I genuinely loved her. Deep down inside I felt like I was never really paid back for breaking her heart in college. In a weird way, maybe I deserved this, but I was going to do the time and pick up the pieces when I got out. Whenever that was.

Chapter 25
The fire burns till the ashes settle

Months had blown by since Conchita left George's penthouse, but she was still devastated by the way he ended it all. She went to Ri-Ri's funeral, but seeing her friend in a coffin began to give her nightmares. *"If I had just taken that package as soon as Deondre' gave it to me, George would've never found out and Ri-Ri would still be alive,"* she thought. Those thoughts were constantly consuming her mind when she was alone. Eventually, Frieda began stacking the appointments up so much that Conchita really didn't think about it often. It was only when she was alone that her demons would haunt her. When she wasn't working she spent a lot of time at late night lounges and local bars trying to 'self-medicate'.

One day, while walking down the street, she began to shiver violently. It *was* forty-five degrees in the fall, but when she stepped inside the local bar she couldn't seemed to shake it off. The shivers got worst. She figured she'd warm up by having a drink, and that the shakes would go away, but they didn't. Trying not to panic, she drank her Tom Collins but began feeling extremely nauseous. Suddenly, she vomited all over the floor.

"Miss, are you okay," the bartender asked.

"Yeah I'm fine. You got a napkin?" she replied wiping the vomit from her lips. He gave her a paper towel and as she wiped her mouth, she quickly closed out her tab. After grabbing her coat, she made her way out the door and back into the cold. She might've gotten three blocks down the street, before her shivers and nausea returned. Trying to stave it off she told herself,

"I'm fine. It's probably something I ate." It wasn't though. All of a sudden, she collapsed on the pavement and into the snow.

When she woke up, she was lying in a hospital bed. Confused as to what had happened, she laid there staring blankly at the television. As soon as she began studying the IV in her arm a doctor entered the room.

"Hi Ms. Roseen, I see you awake," he said jubilantly. Not really in an upbeat mood, she just stared at him scowling.

"I see you're not happy to see me, I wouldn't be either if I woke up here," he said snickering trying to keep the mood upbeat. Growing irritated she snapped,

"Yeah, what the fuck happened?"

"Oh, I see you want me to cut straight to the chase, so I won't hold you up," he quickly replied.

"It seems you were suffering from 'morning sickness' and passed out. Ironic isn't it, considering that it happened at night," he said chuckling. "You felt nauseous and had cold chills, right?" he continued. Before she could reply he blurted out, "Well that's a good thing Ms. Roseen. You're going to be a mommy."

"I guess. How many months am I?" she asked.

"It looks like you're about four or five months along, give or take," he replied. After telling her that, she began doing the math in her head. It wasn't really good news but it wasn't really bad news either. To her, it was just news. She hadn't talked to George in a while, not even once. After he kicked her out, she wanted to call him every day but her pride wouldn't let her. She didn't know how to tell him, even if he did speak to her again.

As she sat and absorbed the information about her newfound pregnancy, suddenly she was hit with a bomb.

"Ms. Roseen, we also ran some test and it seems that you have congenital heart disease. It doesn't look like anything major right now but we'd like to conduct a few more test to decide if you should have surgery or not. It may cause complications when you go to give birth," he said. After he was finished unloading bombs on her, Conchita just sat there stunned. She was now pregnant and diagnosed with heart problems. At first, she thought, *I'll just get an abortion and be done with it.* But as she sat there wondering if George would ever speak to her again she thought, "*If I have it, at least I'd have something to keep us connected.*" While pondering the thought the doctor soon returned with a prescription. He gave her simple instructions about the medication then he casually exited the room. Not wanting to venture back into the cold she figured she stay the night at the hospital and leave in the morning. The next day she begrudgingly stepped out of the hospital bed and proceeded to throw her clothes on. Afterwards, she stopped at the front counter and gave the receptionist her information so that she could be billed, then she quickly left.

As the months drifted along, she noticed her weight picking up. By this time, she had already told Frieda that she was taking a break. Though she had saved up most of her money while escorting, it wasn't enough to buy or rent a place in the city. She didn't want to be alone while she was pregnant either so she eventually moved back in with her mother. Once she settled in, things seemed to be going great. Whenever she needed something her mother was right there to assist her. She seemed to be overjoyed at the fact that Conchita would soon be a mother.

In her ninth month, while she lay on the couch eating a carton of ice cream, she felt a sharp pain in her abdomen. The couch became drenched with fluids and when she stood up, she realized that her water had broken.

"Madre', Madre," Conchita screamed. When her mother heard her, she raced into the living room to see what the problem was. Upon entering the room, she realized that Conchita was going into labor. Soon after, she quickly grabbed her daughter's belongings so that they could head to the hospital. Once they made it to the car, her mother helped her inside and Conchita quickly stretched out across the seats. While cruising down the road, Conchita screamed in agony. Her mother tried comforting her by holding her hand and the stirring wheel, all the while weaving through traffic.

"It's okay baby, we're almost there. Breathe Chi-Chi, breathe," her mother said soothingly. The sound of her mother's voice seemed to take her mind off of the pain and she began breathing with greater ease. Once they arrived at the hospital, her mother hopped out and immediately rushed to help her out of the car. As they scurried up the hospital walk way, the staff realizing that they needed assistance, quickly raced to their aide. Placing Conchita on a stretcher and wheeling her inside.

After Conchita was situated, the nurses urged her to pace her breathing and to push harder. She did as she was directed, but soon begin slipping in and out of consciousness. The intense pain and stress on her body was causing her heart to give out. As soon as she gave her last push, her heart stopped.

"We've lost her," the doctor yelled.

Frantically, they begin trying to resuscitate her. They tried repeatedly but to no avail, it was hopeless. Conchita was gone, and upon hearing that, her mother began to wail hysterically. Not wanting to feel as though their efforts were in vain, the doctor and nurses quickly retrieve the baby from her body. As soon as the baby entered the world, it screamed uncontrollably. Afterwards, the nurses quickly wiped the newborn down and handed it to Conchita's mother.

"Oh, Chi-Chi he's beautiful," she said softly kissing her deceased daughter's cheek. Finally, it was all over. Not just the labor but everything. The turmoil between her and George was over. The mischievous adventures with Ri-Ri were over. The deceit and lies, they were all over.

THE END

Made in the USA
Columbia, SC
15 July 2022

63512239R00126